Forever Amused

SPRING OF LOVE
BOOK TWO

VIRGINIA TAYLOR

Serenade Publishing

Serenade Publishing

www.serenadepublishing.com

Also by Virginia Taylor

Spring of Love Series

Forever Delighted

Forever Amused

Forever Heartfelt

Chapter One

Daisy Gerard sat aiming a deadly stare at her mother, who took absolutely no notice and rose to her feet.

"Well, my dear daughter, I must leave now. The coachman has to drive us to London, and I shouldn't keep him waiting any longer." She shook the hand of Mrs. Toddington, the mother of the new Lord Ashford, and her nearest neighbour. "It's so good of you to have Daisy for the next month. I can't tell you how much I appreciate your offer."

Mrs. Toddington had wonderful manners, because she certainly knew she hadn't offered to have Daisy while the rest of her family went up to town to try find a new husband for Daisy's recently widowed older sister. Mama had clearly baffled the poor woman with her connections between the two families, via uncles way back into the last century until she had finally confused poor Mrs. Toddington enough to say 'yes.' "We are delighted, Lady Gerard."

Hearing this, Daisy should have smiled, but she had planned to be in London, too. A season had been promised to her this year, and now her sister was about to have her second. Instead of impressing Jake Everley with new gowns, Daisy would be stuck in the country with a deadly dull, inarticulate lord and his polite mother.

The only diversion would be the two little girls that Lord Ashford pretended were not his by-blows. Daisy had met them in church a few weeks ago and had taken her mind off the boring sermon by finding the pictures in her hymn book and whispering names for the archangels— naughty names like Camel, Zebra, and Unicorn that made the children giggle.

Mama had nudged her once or twice, but she was used to Daisy and tried her best to ignore her disruptions. Mrs. Toddington had been relieved that the girls had been headed off, and the ridiculous names hadn't turned a single, perfectly groomed hair on her head. Perhaps she was a wicked heathen like Daisy. Daisy hoped so, or she would wilt for the next few days while she had plotted her escape.

Finally, she saw off her mother, and trudged back with Mrs. Toddington into the stately manor house, newly acquired by the seventh earl of Ashford. "Perhaps I ought unpack." A pointless exercise in her opinion, for she would soon need to pack up again.

"Let me show you to your room." Mrs. Toddington, who had to be at least in her forties, had pure white skin, enormous dark eyes, and chestnut curls, dressed high. She wore a simple green round gown with an exotic shawl draped stylishly over her elbows.

Daisy followed her silent hostess up the wide staircase,

wondering how on earth she would fill her life while she sat bored out of her mind, when she should have been having her season in London. Coming from a boisterous family, she was accustomed to noise and botheration, much of which was her contribution. Her time with the restrained Ashford family would be deadly dull. The whole place needed livening up, in her opinion.

As for Lord Ashford, well, he wasn't even handsome. He was disgustingly pretty with his big brown eyes, curly dark hair any woman would kill for, and eyelashes that she didn't want to even look at because they were so effeminate. And dimples. Dimples! Good God. The whole man was a waste of the makings of a gorgeous woman, except he was far too tall, with wide shoulders, slim hips, and long muscular legs. The next few days would be horrendous and the worst punishment ever inflicted on Daisy.

However, within a week, she planned be on her way to London, where she would make wild promises about behaving herself. She sat plotting on her bed for a good ten minutes, before she heard a timid knock on her door. Arising, she began to pick through her clothes as if she meant to unpack. A maid entered. "I'm Smithson and I will be your maid while you're here," said the woman in a nervous voice.

Daisy stepped aside, crossing her arms, while the chubby creature, who would be in her late twenties, began to stack Daisy's sparse wardrobe on the bed. "I don't need help, Smithson, other than hot water in the morning. I know how to unpack my valise."

"I expect you'll be wanting your hair done, though," Smithson said with a dour glance at the bird's nest Daisy normally wore, Daisy didn't care how her ghastly hair looked. Long ago, she had realised that no one could make the curly wisps look thick and lustrous. Therefore, she made a high pile of her hair, which normally collapsed early in the day. "You could do with a tidy-up."

Daisy laughed. "This is about as tidy as my hair can be."

Smithson eyed her. "Likely, it doesn't matter. The master isn't one to notice."

Which confirmed Daisy's opinion of Lord Ashford. He wouldn't glance twice at her. In town, he would be much admired for his girlish looks, but in the country he had to rest on his merits as a landowner, and his lands were in a right old mess. Most of the stock had been sold off by the previous Lord Ashford and the locals expected the new one to begin selling off more land, as each earl before him had done.

After her clothes had been neatly placed in the drawers, now that she had been organised, she had no choice other than to return to the drawing room. She sat with Mrs. Toddington. As her hostess seemed inclined to keep asking questions, Daisy put her mind to the local gossip. She knew all the recent scandals and relished the retelling. She got to the Warren family, whose oafish son had emptied a cartload of pebbles in the main street, thinking he might fill up a pot-hole or two, when a large shadow loomed in the doorway.

Mrs. Toddington glanced over Daisy's head with a tender smile on her face. "I wondered where you had gone, my dear," she said to her son as he entered the room. "I thought you would remember we were expecting a house-guest today. Have you met Miss Daisy Gerard?"

Daisy rose to her feet to curtsey to Lord Ashford. "I'm

not sure we have been formally introduced, though of course I have seen you in the village, my lord."

He nodded, which appeared to be his best acknowledgement of her words. If she had been her sister, Corinne, she would have swooned. Close up, the man was every maiden's dream. His build was even more marvellous than at a distance, almost intimidating. He stripped off his hat and gloves and turned to place them in the waiting footman's hands. "Miss Gerard," he said in a remote voice. "Delighted."

"That's fortunate, because you have me for the next four weeks. I have promised Mama not to be a pest and to help wherever I can." She clasped her hands neatly in front, and offered a copy of her sister's best melting expression.

His eyebrows drew together, and he leaned back as if affronted. Most people reacted with pleasure when she acted angelic. He appeared not to care. In which case, they would get on superbly. She wouldn't need to waste her precious time trying to impress him. He quickly averted his gaze. For a moment, a touch of self-consciousness overcame her and she wondered if her hair looked worse than usual, and actually put up her fingers to touch the bird's nest. He noted her action and she raised her chin in a challenge to him.

"I'm sure you will be a great help," Lord Pretty Face said in a disinterested voice.

"Yes, I'm sure I will." She knew she wouldn't.

"Your sister is in town, I hear?"

"Both my sisters are in town."

"I have only been introduced to Corinne," Mrs.

Toddington said, the expression on her face concerned. "She is a very young widow, isn't she?"

"She has always been lucky."

Mrs. Toddington blinked and stared at her. "Did she make a bad marriage?" she asked in a careful voice.

"I don't think she is as choosy as I am. She wasn't willing to wait for a better offer."

Lord Ashford glanced at her, his expression unreadable.

"Her dear departed had sandy hair." Daisy used her saintly tone, since he hadn't reacted to her remark with either a smile or rank disapproval.

"How unwise," he said gently.

Suspicious, she caught his gaze, but the block appeared to be serious. "It's best to keep one's standards high."

He and his mother exchanged glances. Daisy laughed inside. Within a day she would be sent on her way. The longer Corinne had with Jake unsupervised by her second sister, the more likely that he wouldn't notice Corinne's faults. He was far more influenced by women's looks than he ought to be. In the meantime, Daisy had to continue being annoying or she would be stuck here for the whole summer.

Lord Ashford turned away and disappeared.

She turned back to Mrs. Toddington. "A man of few words."

Mrs. Toddington nodded. "Perhaps he needed to see to the girls."

"I was hoping to see them, too."

"They'll be down before dinner. They eat early and come to say goodnight before they go to bed. We eat early in the country, and dinner will be served around six, if that will suit you."

Daisy wasn't planning on being a too inconvenient guest and six suited her. Then she could have an early night and arise as soon as the sun did. Finally, she ran out of boring gossip and went up to her room to change for dinner, wondering how she would fill tomorrow now that she had exhausted every subject women were expected to talk about.

If she had been in the city with her family, she would have plenty to do, what with the shops and the visiting and seeing Jake, who was her dearest love... as well as being the reason she was being kept from town.

Tired, tired of being saddled with debts, other people's children, tired of not managing, the earl went to his suite to exchange his old jacket and breeches for evening wear. His valet had put out his selections, black and black. Supposedly, Ashford was mourning for the last earl, from whom he had unexpectedly inherited his depleted estate.

The earldom had passed through the hands of two earls in the last four years. Each had done his best to sell off most of the stock. All that remained were the entailed properties, leaving Ashford with nothing except vacant fields, decrepit fences, and weeds. He had also inherited two children, who seemed to be his second cousins. Their own mother had disappeared a few months ago and no other home had been found for them yet. He'd been told their remaining grandparents were in no position to take two children, and had suggested placement in

7

an orphanage. If Ashford couldn't pan them off to some other relative, he would have to keep them. He found the idea of sending two innocent children off to an orphanage repellent.

For this reason, his mother had been trying harder than ever before to marry him off to money. Her goal hadn't and wouldn't change, but he had only ever been in love once. His dream wife had married the wild Lord Delmore. Clearly, a man as reserved as Ashford wouldn't have been a good match for her. Although couldn't see past his heartache, he needed a mother for the girls, perhaps an older woman. He couldn't saddle a young lady with children, when she would clearly prefer her own.

Thudding back down the main stairs two by two, he managed to escape to his study before anyone accosted him. Studying the debts had become his main occupation, since gazing at the unplanted fields depressed him. Fortunately, he had learned land management from all the conversations participated in by young wealthy men at Oxford. That or wine, women, and song, which he also enjoyed, especially the singing part. Strangely, he didn't stutter when he sang and, in fact, he rarely stuttered these days.

A shadow passed his study door and returned in the elegant shape of his mother. "There you are, my dear. I have been searching for you, everywhere."

He smiled, knowing he was rarely *everywhere*. "'Hide in plain sight' should be on the family coat of arms," he answered mildly. "It seems to be what I do best."

As a former stutterer, Ashford had found life easier if he remained in the background. When he had spoken, he'd had to concentrate very long and hard before beginning.

This meant that other people took up the habit of starting or finishing his sentences. For this reason, he never made himself the centre of attention. In large groups he was invariably overlooked. Every now and again in moments of stress, the fault appeared back in his speech. At Eton he had been called t-t-Toddie.

"I wanted to tell you to take no notice of Miss Gerard. According to her mother, she is a little upset because she expected to be presented this year."

"Instead she is hidden away with us."

Mama heaved sigh. "Yes, dear. Her elder sister was widowed a year ago. She has just come out of mourning and Lady Gerard wants to support her during her re-entrance into society."

Ashford stared at his mother. "It seems a little unfair, don't you think?"

"It works well for us, because she likes Dawn and Eve. And we need someone to help us with them. And she wouldn't expect a wage." The smile she offered looked guilty.

So, that was the young lady's appeal. Poor mother. After living on a small stipend for many years, she couldn't accustom herself to being better off now that her only child had inherited the earldom. "It won't be a much fun for her, when she was expecting the delights of the season." He couldn't imagine what a spirited young lady would find interesting about spending part of her day with a five and a six year-old, and the other part with an unsociable bachelor -- who preferred peace and quiet -- and his mother. But no doubt Mother had the whole matter in hand. She appeared to think so, for she disappeared without a further comment.

He managed to balance the books, with a little left over to hire another labourer for the home farm. A married couple managed to supply the manor with butter and milk, and cream on a good day. They decided that a chicken run would be a good idea. This is how Ashford spent his days, on trivialities like the price of eggs, or how many cabbages he could grow per square foot. Finally, the dinner gong sounded.

And what a treat awaited him before dinner: two chatting ladies and two shrill-voiced little girls. He pasted on his unruffled expression. "Good evening, ladies."

Miss Gerard offered one of her curtsies. He wondered if he had met her before and wasn't remembering. He knew her family well enough, having been at Eton and Cambridge with her short and charming brother, who hadn't been among his tormentors at school. As for Miss Gerard, she stood as tall as her brother, but she was half a head shorter than Ashford's six-foot height.

On his second examination of her face, he doubted he had met her before. He wouldn't have forgotten her. She wasn't what he would call pretty but her face was interesting. Her sister had soft blonde hair and a sweet, rather doll-like face. Miss Daisy Gerard had a smile that she used deliberately, not necessarily to charm, but to fix a man in the eye and tell him she expected to be bored. Her eyes were large and intensely green, and her hair seemed to be a dark gold. He wasn't good at describing colours but he would venture to guess her hair would be called brassy.

He also ventured to guess that his mother would call

the young lady brassy as well. After another glance at her calculating expression, he would say she was a handful. He decided he shouldn't smile companionably at her, although he was glad she already liked the children. Adopting his bland expression, he indicated the chair behind her. "You have become reacquainted with my little girls?" he said carefully.

She nodded. "The girls have been entertaining us with stories, haven't you, sweethearts?"

The sweethearts, Dawn and Eve, looked defensive. Neither spoke. Par for the course. "I would like them to tell me stories too, but I haven't been lucky so far. One day, perhaps."

Eve pulled at Dawn's sleeve.

Dawn took a deep breath and faced him. "We told her that we saw a monster lizard once."

Ashford sent a querying glance to Miss Gerard.

She nodded. "A very large lizard, wasn't it, sweethearts?"

Eve put a thumb in her mouth and Dawn nodded. "We need to draw one for her, Miss Gerard said."

Ashford glanced at his mother. "Do we have any lizards here?"

She appeared puzzled. "I doubt it. Sightings are rare. But they used to live in the heath lands. Off to bed, now, girls."

After the nursery maid had removed the children, Ashford turned to Miss Gerard. "The girls appear to like you."

She shrugged. "I said I would teach them to draw. Dawn wants to learn letters too, but I told them we are all

11

having a summer break. That's because I have no idea how to teach letters, but I like to draw." She shrugged.

He glanced at her mother who had a wry expression on her face. "I'm sure Lord Ashford will be delighted if you keep his girls happy, no matter how."

"Indeed. And I expect I will need to interview their nurse as to l-learning their l-letters." He clamped his lips shut. The stutter came when he worried. He tried to empty his mind and turned away, pretending he wanted a glass of Madeira.

"I expect it's not my place to speak to the nurse about their education," Miss Daisy said in a speculative tone. "But perhaps I could help out a little."

"How kind," his mother said in her company voice. "Shall we go into dinner now?"

Daisy tossed and turned that night, thinking about Corinne. Although Mama thought her older daughter deserved sympathy, and Daisy didn't disagree, her sister had already had her turn. She should have told Mama that, instead of expecting the world to revolve around her sad life. Daisy also had a sad life.

She'd been Jake's supporter forever and she'd watched from the sidelines while he flirted his way around society, never taking responsibility for anything he did. He'd broken more hearts than Daisy could count, but she had always assumed he was waiting for her grow old enough to marry. She'd been old enough for the past three years. He still had a mistress and hadn't offered for anyone.

Two weeks ago, she'd heard Mama muttering about Corinne, who had been widowed last year, after two years of marriage. Corinne had always expected to marry Jake, but Lord Standing had offered for her first. Thankfully, or Daisy would have needed to kill her sister, who had decided long ago to marry Jake, not because she adored him, but because she thought she could change him into the perfect husband.

Daisy had no intention of changing a man who was already perfect for her. He laughed at her jokes, he indulged her whims, and he was always available when she needed someone with whom to share her innermost secrets. The only one she had never told him was that she loved him.

Her plan, during her season in London, had been to show him that she was ready for marriage. More than ready, being almost twenty-one. But now she was imprisoned in Ashford's country house while Corinne was having her second chance to trap the man Daisy would die for.

Her throat ached, her head ached, and she wished she had the ability to behave like a demure and respectable young lady. Tears began to stream from her eyes. She wished she always knew the right words to say, she wished she had charm and style, and she wished she had never offended a single person in her whole life. Instead, she fell into one scrape after another.

When she was younger, her disruptions hadn't bothered Jake. He had indulged Daisy's every whim since she was ten. If she was angry, he would listen to her gripes, if she was sad, he would take her fishing or for a march across the fields, or even riding if Mama let her go. He always laughed at her silly jokes. When she was fifteen, he made sure of dancing with her upstairs when Mama hadn't let her go down to the ballroom.

Jake was charming and kind and tall and good looking. She had decided to marry him as soon as she grew old enough. But he still treated her like a fifteen year-old, and she'd wanted to prove she was old enough.

And she had been caught, awaiting him in his bed.

Unfortunately, he hadn't been in Huntsdale House as the time, and the duchess, Cassia, had found her and dragged her off to speak to her mother.

At first she had thought she would be locked in her room for a year, and starved to death. But, no. She had to stay in the country while Corinne was given her second chance to capture Jake instead, while Daisy had to spend her time with a tall boring earl, his nice mother, and two perky little girls.

Chapter Two

After arising bright and early the next morning, Daisy formulated her evil plan. She hauled a blue cotton gown out from the drawer, placed her undergarments on the bed, and brushed out her sleeping plait. This morning she had much to do and no time to waste since she wanted to make sure she would be dispatched to her family in the city as soon as possible.

She planned to be an interfering busybody. People who offered needless help and took over other people's lives drove her insane. No doubt, she could be the world's greatest pest, and so annoying that she would be asked to leave very soon. The little girls fit nicely into her plan. She grinned as she rang for the maid. Interfering with the nursery routine like a regular know-all would certainly be the best way to wear out her welcome.

Despite the brilliance of her plan, she experienced an amount of sympathy for unsuspecting Mrs. Toddington, who seemed very nice. The poor woman hadn't deserved to be lumped with Daisy, whose season in London was currently being usurped by her sister. Without a doubt, Corinne would take advantage of the fact the Jake always fell for the wrong females. His family wanted him married off to a suitable woman, and saintly Corrine would be seen as perfect foil for a lord with licentious ways. But despite his constantly scandalous behaviour, Jake didn't deserve to be punished by marriage to a prosy bore. If he married Daisy, she could divert him from his drinking and gambling and making merry with ladies of the night, by being a loving wife.

Her bedroom door opened. "Your hot water, Miss." Smithson busied into the room, placing the bowl on the washstand in the corner.

"Thank you, Smithson. What time do they serve the nursery breakfast?"

"Seven o'clock, Miss, the same time as the master and mistress. Mrs. Templeton is already at the table."

"I'll be downstairs in less than two minutes if you can lace my gown for me."

Smithson bobbed a curtsey and wasted no time in chatter. Since Mama had decided that Daisy would wear pale blue this season, this allowed her to step-up from the pink she had worn the year before. She had finished settling all her layers while helped with the hooks and then she dashed downstairs to the breakfast room.

Mrs. Toddington sat alone, looking wonderful in the severe shade of gray she wore. Although probably in her late forties, she had perfected her posture and kept a willowy figure, unlike Daisy's mother who was rather dumpy. Lord Ashford was no doubt still sleeping off his lack of activity of the day before.

"Good morning," Daisy said, trying to sound perky, although she felt a tinge of guilt. Coming from a large family, she had never eaten alone in her whole life, and she pitied poor Mrs. Toddington. Had Daisy known the earl would not be present, she would have joined her solitary hostess earlier.

Mrs. Toddington smiled. "Do sit and have a breakfast with me. My son just left. He is an early riser and had business to attend."

Daisy blinked and stared at a table beautifully set with floral china. The silver warming dishes sat centrally. She helped herself to a dish of eggs, eying the thin slices of ham while a servant poured a cup of coffee for her. "Do you have plans for me today?"

"What would you like to do?"

"I should see to Dawn and Eve. After all, I did promise that we could draw."

"I'm sure they would love to see you. They don't have any company other than the Earl and me, and I can't spend all day adoring them. They need occupation and being closer to them in age, I'm sure you can find a few things to do that might interest them, aside from drawing."

"I'm sure I can." Daisy's younger days had been mainly spent outdoors. She would have been disgusted if she had to study all day. "We could start with a nature walk. That's what my nursery maid called playing hide and seek in the garden or climbing trees."

Mrs. Toddington laughed. "I'm sure she had her hands full with three of you. You are a dear girl. Thank you so much. My son and I aren't used to children."

In which case Lord Ashford should have kept his falls

buttoned. A fat lot of use he was as a father, when he didn't even acknowledge his relationship to Dawn and Eve. As his bastards, they should have a better life than being locked up in nursery with a maid who couldn't even keep them neat and tidy. The dresses they had worn last night had badly stitched hems and absolutely no trimmings. As the by-blows of an earl, they should have an education and a chance to marry well. "The neighbours would be delighted to play with them if you arranged to have them brought here."

"Would the children of the neighbours be suitable companions for our ... wards?"

Daisy nodded. "They were suitable for us. We had friends in high and low places. Children are children after all."

"Yes." Mrs. Toddington looked thoughtful. "I could perhaps arrange something of the kind."

"The district didn't even know you had children here until a few weeks ago when they appeared in church."

Mrs. Toddington gave a guilty smile. "I had only known of their existence a few weeks before that. The woman who had been caring for them contacted Ashford after the old earl died. After that, Ashford decided to give them a home here."

Daisy stared at her plate, trying to keep her expression blank. *The woman who had been caring for them only contacted their father after the old earl died?* Her lip curled with disbelief. 'The woman might be able to forgive him one child, but she shouldn't have forgiven him two. She should have told him about the second instantly, instead of trying to hide both her children. The shame should not rest only on the mother's shoulders. Half the input came from the father. Ashford should have been supporting them from day one, no matter his position.

Others might see bringing them to his country house as praiseworthy. Not Daisy. She only had to think about his innocent daughters to realise why his good looks would never make an impression on her. Picking up her fork, she hoped she wouldn't choke on her disgust about his behaviour. She wouldn't excuse him for ignoring them until he had inherited a title.

If he made the slightest effort, he would be quite popular among the locals—despite his immorality—being fit and healthy and unlikely to turn up his toes as quickly as the last two. The previous holder of the title hadn't been inclined to socialise with the neighbours, and then he promptly died, leaving himself largely unknown. She stuffed her eggs into her mouth and had barely swallowed her last mouthful before Smithson entered the room.

"Miss Gerard asked me to tell her when the children's breakfast was being served," Smithson said hesitantly to Mrs. Toddington with a curtsey.

"I wanted to be shown the way to the nursery, but I couldn't inflict myself on the girls until they had eaten." Daisy stood.

Mrs. Toddington nodded and smiled, and Daisy marched back up the stairs to find a kitchen maid awaiting her with a breakfast tray. Her thoughts switched from Ashford, and began to focus on her plans to escape this house. She dutifully followed the maid along the passage to another flight of stairs that led to an attic nursery. She opened the door for the maid and stopped dead in her tracks.

The room was in a state of chaos. Books lay opened on the floor, torn pages scattered far and wide. A circle of dolls, most disabled by missing limbs or hair, was surrounded by a box of assorted toys. Two little girls in creased white cotton nightgowns sat ready at the table staring at the empty plates in front of them. Tangled dark hair wafted around two suspiciously innocent faces.

"Good morning, dear ones. What happened in here? Did a naughty fairy come into the room and wave her wand to make this mess?"

Two pairs of wary eyes stared at her while the maid placed the breakfast tray on the centre of the table and backed toward the door without a word. Another door opened on the left side of the room. A short and dumpy woman in her early twenties came scurrying in. She looked as unkempt as the girls, dressed in a gown of striped cotton twill, her cheeks a flustered red, and her mousy hair tied with a thin ribbon at the end of scrawny plait. "Good morning, Miss. Don't you trouble yourself. I'll get these children fed."

Daisy walked forward and offered her hand for a quick shake. "Good morning. I'm Daisy Gerard, and I presume you are the children's nurse?"

The woman flicked back her plait. "Mary is my name, Miss. I'm the nursery maid." She stood with what Daisy read as a watchful expression on her face.

Daisy nodded. "I'm sure breakfast can wait until the girls are properly dressed."

Mary blinked, her face a picture of affront. "These

naughty girls don't give me time, Miss. Up all night playing around with the toys, they were, no matter how many times I put them back into bed."

Two little foreheads creased, while the girls watched the to and fro of the conversation.

"Don't worry, Mary. I will see to the girls. Now, sweet ones, we will get you washed and dressed, too."

The children slid off their chairs and slunk into a room on the right. Knowing that little girls needed help to dress, Daisy followed into a bedroom that was as messy as the nursery. The pillows had been placed on the floor and surrounded with the bed covers. Apparently, a nest had been needed sometime during the night. "Did the maid forget to bring your washing water?"

Dawn nodded. "Mary doesn't worry about washing before breakfast, you know. She says she likes to eat first."

"Ladies always wash first thing in the morning," Daisy said in a serious voice. "We will do that now because your breakfast is waiting." Having finished her old nurse's dictums, Daisy turned to Mary, who stood with her hands clasped together and her eyes as large as a dinner plates. "Bring washing bowls for the girls, please, and quickly."

The maid nodded and scurried out of the room.

Noting that Eve couldn't manage her own hair, Daisy brushed the smaller child's hair. Dawn brushed her own, none too well, and not with any great enthusiasm, mumbling about why she didn't want to wash and dress. By the time both girls were tangle-free, the water had been delivered. Mary helped by washing Dawn, and a light gown was tossed over each of two small heads.

Approximately fifteen minutes after the breakfast had

been brought up, the group sat at the nursery table, two silently, and one resentfully. The last, Daisy, lowered herself a little tentatively, worrying that she may have been a little abrupt.

The girls consumed their milk pudding, and shared an apple Daisy cut into pieces for them. "What shall we do next, dear ones?"

Two little girls and one sulky nursemaid stared at her.

"What do you normally do, Mary?"

Mary shrugged. "They're dressed. They can play now."

At least they were fed and watered. "Perhaps you should say good morning to Lord Ashford and Mrs. Toddington?"

Eve nudged Dawn, who said, "We don't usually. We play with the dolls or we go outside with Mary to talk to the grooms."

Mary managed a light puff of laughter. "We do a little drawing after playtime, don't we girls?"

Eve stared out the window while Dawn stared at her plate. "I would like to learn how to read, Miss Daisy," she mumbled, raising her gaze. She had pretty brown eyes like Lord Ashford's. "Will I be able to, if I draw first?"

Daisy blinked. For her, drawing had been the first essential in her life. "You don't have to draw if you don't wish to, Dawn. Do you know your letters?"

Dawn nodded. "Eve doesn't. Eve, do you want to draw or learn your letters?"

Eve's gaze lifted from her empty plate and stared at the fragments of apple-core on the stacked dishes.

"She would like more apple," Dawn said softly.

"I'm sure more fruit can be arranged. I'll return after I have spoken with Mrs. Toddington."

Not having expected to organise the children's dietary requirements, nor their whole education, Daisy needed to think. The menu would be straight forward, but school-room routine would be complicated. The older child wanted to read and write. The younger didn't speak. Daisy didn't know what they did all day, other than to talk to the grooms. Surely a governess should be employed? Or at least, a nanny. However, she couldn't tell Mrs. Toddington her business, and Daisy's tact was about as well-developed as her charm.

Her shoulders sagging, she began to pick through the cupboards until she found the pencils and paper.

Ashford was glad not to have seen Miss Gerard at breakfast. He already had two female youngsters to look after. The third didn't interest him in the least. He didn't doubt she would be primping at her hair and deciding how low to take her neckline after she had noted his disinterest. Females seemed to want his attention, but the reason why was beyond him. He had absolutely no conversation, a modest income, and his greatest fear was going into an incoherent stutter when asked a question. That was in the past, he hoped, but the ever-present fear had made him into a silent observer.

This young lady had been banished from London for the season. He could only presume, since she didn't appear to have the measles, or be anything other than in perfect health, that she was being separated from an unwise alliance. Whether he and his mother were the appropriate people to shelter her would remain to be seen.

He eyed the pile of correspondence in front of him and sighed deeply. Reaching out, he took his pen in hand. After working at his desk until the sun sat higher than the trees in the skyline, he emerged from his study, having sent off his weasel-worded letters to cattle breeders who had sturdy stock for sale, and having paid a few outstanding bills.

After flexing his arms above his head, he wandered out into the garden where he spotted his mother. "What amusements have we arranged for Miss Gerard while she is here?" He strolled towards her. Bees circled around him, buzzing faintly.

She turned to him, placing a branch of thorny roses into her gardening basket. The day was fine and bright, and the flowers had bloomed, but like everything else on the property, the garden hadn't been well maintained. His mother was attempting to rectify this particular problem.

"I presume she is still with the children," his mother said in her usual thoughtful way. She had been widowed by the time he had turned twenty-two years old, and by choice, had kept her single state. He didn't doubt she'd had offers because she had kept her looks. Not only did she have large brown eyes, a slim straight nose, and a mouth that smiled without restraint, her dark hair held few grey strands and her body remained slim and active. Of course, she knew how to dress to flatter, although short of money, but best of all, she had the kindest heart of anyone he knew. She even kindly chopped off the head of a blown white rose. "Perhaps later, she could help me with the invitations for my card evening." Her eyes met his, as if in query.

"I think she may need more amusement than addressing envelopes." He aimed his gaze into the distance, focusing on the higher buildings in the village, spotting the spire of the parish church. "Do we have any local entertainments?"

She furrowed her brow. "Miss Gerard knows the district better than we do. You could ask her."

"I suppose I should."

"Are you planning to stay here, Ashford? I thought you would go back to the city for the rest of the season."

"I had planned to, yes, but I'd as soon spend time here. I don't know the place well, and I have many changes I would like to make. And, of course, tenants who might like to have my ear."

"Assuming you still plan to find an heiress, you would be better off in London during the season." She snipped off another perfect long-stemmed rose and placed the bloom in her basket.

"Possibly, but I haven't found an heiress during this past year that hasn't been scooped up by a fellow with far more address than I can summon up. If I can get this place up and running, I won't need an heiress."

"Your father discovered it's not easy to run a large estate without the backing of money." Mother half smiled, but she was softening the blow. She didn't think he knew how to do anything but silently decorate balls and soirees and garden parties.

Until recently, his only talent had been heiress-hunting, which he managed badly. He would get to the point of being about to make an offer, and then be put off by a lack of kindness, or a lack of taste, or a lack of not being the

25

woman he loved. A quiet life on his small country estate would have suited him well enough, but he wanted to share that with a compatible partner who could love him for himself rather than the way he looked. He had been in line for the earldom, but no one ever imagined that the three ahead of him would pass into the next world like a stack of falling domino tiles.

"Perhaps not, but I had a good education that I don't plan to waste." He glanced around, appreciating the garden and the work his mother was doing to re-establish the beds. "This is a sound property that has been left to run wild, with so many new owners in such a short time."

He drifted off, uncertain whether to approach Miss Gerard or to find his steward. Miss Gerard lost. He trudged up to the nursery wing, a dank echoing space filled with all the old furniture in the house. Low-toned voices drew him to the room, where the two little girls were seated at the nursery table.

Miss Gerard sat on a tiny chair at the other side of the table, facing them. "The letters of the alphabet are now on the chalkboard. I want you to say the ones you know."

As he entered the room, Miss Gerard turned to him with lifted eyebrows. "Good morning, my lord."

"Is it still morning? In that case, good morning, Miss Gerard. Good morning Miss Dawn and Miss Eve."

Eve gave him a quick glance of recognition.

Dawn offered him a shy smile. "May we go outside to play, now, sir?"

"I believe Miss Gerard gave you a condition to fulfil. Eve may try the letters first." Rather than sit on the sidelines like an authentic earl, he gingerly settled himself on a nursery chair beside Miss Gerard, his chin almost touching his knees. Miss Gerard eyed him with a frown. Her chair squeaked on the wooden floor as she edged her chair away from him.

Eve stared as if he had grown horns out of his head.

Dawn said, "Bh for bat. Ff for frog. Huh for horse."

Miss Daisy nodded. "Very good."

Dawn concentrated. "Gh for good."

"Wonderful. Your turn Eve."

"Eve doesn't know them, Miss Daisy. I will do them all but you didn't draw a picture for X and so I don't know a word that might be right."

"I expect Lord Ashford could tell you." Miss Daisy shot a smug glance at him."

"X is a letter we rarely use. I think you can learn it just in case. Now, I believe I promised to take two children outside. Are you wanting to climb trees or should I take you to the dairy?"

The little girls smiled. "No, sir," answered the designated spokes-girl. "Perhaps we could offer hay to the horses so that one day they would like us and take us galloping over the hills."

"That's a mighty good idea."

Miss Daisy folded her arms across her chest and lowered her eyebrows. "They're too young to go galloping over the hills. If you don't mind, I will stay up here while they pat the horses. I'm sure Mary would be very happy to go with you."

He wondered if she disliked horses, but that was a subject for another day. "I'm sure none of us mind, Miss Gerard. I know my mother would love your company." He stood and offered his hand to help her stand, which she took with what appeared to be resentment. Perhaps he had hurt her feelings by removing his small relatives from her for a while. He offered her what he hoped was a pleasant smile to soften the blow.

For a moment, her eyes narrowed as if she was trying to take his measure. Then, she apparently came to the conclusion that doing as he wished would be easier than trying to think of an excuse. "I would be delighted. Thank you, my lord."

When she smiled, her whole face lit up. Her eyes filled with mischief and her cheeks rounded like ripe peaches. He momentarily responded with an intake of breath. Beneath that possibly justified resentment lurked a young lady who knew how to confuse a fellow with her moods.

He held out a hand for Dawn and Eve, who clasped him carefully. After previously noting how cautious they were about accepting his overtures, he tried to be aware that in the past few years they had been passed from one relative to another, and had been let down each time. "Shall we visit the apple orchard before we see the horses?"

"Miss Daisy said Eve could have an apple, but she didn't get one."

Miss Daisy shot him a wide-eyed glance. "I'm so sorry, Eve. Never let me break a promise. Remind me, as you did."

Eve stood, examining the expression on the young lady's face, and finally offered a quick nod of acceptance. Hats and coats being unnecessary in this late spring weather, he expected to leave instantly, but Eve raced into the bedroom for a fluffy ball, which she pushed into her apron pocket. Dawn frowned at her.

He led the three downstairs. Miss Daisy asked for directions to his mother and the little girls ranged either side of him, skipping along at his side.

Daisy, her hand shading her eyes against the sun, found Mrs. Toddington in the garden as promised by Lord Ashford, filling her basket with the new roses. "I believe you might have a few tasks for me," she called as she approached.

"We were thinking you might like to go to the assemblies in Guildford." Mrs. Toddington raised her gaze, resting her garden scissors in her rapidly filling basket. "Ashford should certainly attend. He barely knows any of the neighbours. For the past three months, since taking possession of Ashford Hall, he has been travelling back and forth to London, and he barely knows anyone here—other than your dear parents, of course."

"Does he plan to stay in the country?" Daisy's throat dried as she tried to sound unconcerned. "My brother never remains here during the season. Too much fun in town, he always says. The assemblies here are very tame affairs, smallish, held in a room purpose-built off the local inn."

"I expect he will like that." Mrs. Toddington put her shears in her basket and began stripping off her leather gloves. "He appears to prefer the smaller events."

"Here, let me take that basket from you. I hope this won't be my only task. Lord Ashford decided to escort the children to the stables, leaving me with nothing to do."

Mrs. Toddington handed over her basket and began to

walk along the green edged path back to the house. "I would really like to have a little gathering here, too, so that Ashford can meet the neighbours properly."

"Most of the landed gentry are in the city at this time of year." Daisy hoped she sounded nonchalant. Even the smallest distraction like busybody neighbours would threaten her plan to escape.

Mrs. Toddington caught her gaze. "Do you think we won't be able to get up enough people for a supper dance?" she asked, sounding disappointed.

Daisy didn't want to see her neighbours. Everyone would wonder why she was staying with the newest family in the district rather than being in London. Although she had an inventive mind, she honestly didn't want to talk about herself or her life with anyone. "I expect we could find the numbers you might want," she said with reluctance.

"And will you help me with the invitations?" Mrs. Toddington's gaze caught hers as she turned onto the carriage sweep.

Daisy didn't want to help. She didn't want to stay. She also couldn't be so ungracious as to refuse her help to a woman who had, without a single question, had taken her in. "Of course I will," she said with a deflation of her chest. "But might I suggest that we attend an assembly first? That will let everyone know that Lord Ashford is at home, and the neighbours will come calling soon after."

"Well, that's the very thing we ought do. Unless Ashford hasn't paid for a subscription to the assembly rooms."

"I expect he has," Daisy said, blithely. Even if he hadn't,

someone would drop enough hints after they arrived to tactfully let him know. No one would refuse entrance to an earl. "I don't have a full wardrobe with me, but I wasn't expecting any formal events. I can go home and find a few more outfits, if need be."

"We will send for your gowns if you wish. Your mother said she had left the house staffed. You don't need to put yourself to the trouble. I wish I'd had a daughter. I would have loved to bring one out. Your mother is so lucky to have three of you."

"And to bring one of us out twice?" Daisy said in an undertone. Her eyebrows lifted with the disdain she felt for her mother's appalling decision. Her gaze briefly met Mrs. Toddington's.

Mrs. Toddington stopped. She frowned. "Is she doing so because your sister was widowed?"

"Apparently Cornelia mustn't be left on the shelf at her age." Daisy watched the swing of the flower basket in her hand.

"I sympathise with that thought. I didn't have a mother when my husband died and I had a baby son who needed me. How old is your sister?"

"Cornelia is twenty-four. She had two seasons before she accepted her marriage offer. I had to wait for her to wed before I came out. Then her husband died. We all, our family, went into mourning with her. So, my own come-out has been delayed by some years."

Mrs. Toddington took her hand and squeezed. "I hope we can make your stay with us an adequate substitute. Perhaps she will meet her next husband this week and you will be able to go back and have your own season."

The lady's instant understanding caused Daisy's eyes to gloss over. She blinked away the thought of tears. "I pray she will meet someone suitable and if she could possibly do that in a week, I would be amazed. You know how it is in society. We all know each other, or at least, *of* each other. I can only hope someone new enters the scene."

"You are a dear girl to care so much for your sister's happiness."

Daisy squared her shoulders. For the first time in her life she was congratulated, but for the wrong reason. She didn't care if Cornelia found a husband or not. She'd had her turn and she should let Daisy have hers. So, for all the times she had not been congratulated when she deserved praise, she smiled as if she deserved acknowledgement. "In the meantime, we will plan our visit to take the assembly rooms by storm."

"By storm?" Mrs. Toddington said with a slow, mischievous smile. "Let's do it gently and in style and save the storm for our first supper dance here."

Daisy smiled and swung the basket all the way back to the house. Perhaps the next few days wouldn't be as dull as she had expected. At least she could look forward to a night of dancing with her local friends rather than sitting idle and bored.

Ashford returned the girls to the nursery maid, having discovered why the visit to the stables had been so imperative. Kittens. The best mouse-catcher ever seen in these parts had produced a litter of five smoky eyed, tawny kittens. These little sharp-toothed, needle-clawed creatures had swarmed around his feet and caught at the skirts of the girls, who squealed with delight. He had needed to do nothing more than sit on a bale of hay watching them, to be pronounced the mostest bestest person in the whole of England.

The apples and cores had been tossed into the stalls, the horses not being any attraction at all. He didn't need to think about buying a couple of ponies for a while yet.

The nursery maid had tidied the room by the time they returned, and she sat them down with pencils and paper. She mentioned lunch and they looked happy enough. He always had paperwork waiting for him in his study. The life of an earl wasn't all playing with kittens and worrying about little girls.

He sighed and went back downstairs.

Chapter Three

Daisy trudged back to the nursery. Mrs. Toddington's offer to let her help with organising a supper party sounded interesting. If Daisy could be of use, she would be honoured. In her own home, she was superfluous, not being the darling oldest daughter or the precious younger daughter. In fact, her banishment from town life wouldn't be quite as awful as she had expected.

She rather admired Mrs. Toddington, who was an accepting sort of woman, not prone to fussing overmuch about anything. Aside from that, she was elegant, which Daisy's mother was decidedly not. Mama tried so hard to dress her daughters in the latest styles, but Daisy always felt awkward in lace and frills. She could never quite put her finger on why her gowns appeared to hide her. Mrs. Toddington wore gowns in brighter colours with more style than flounces. She would be Daisy's pattern card.

Beginning to cheer up, she re-entered the nursery. Dawn and Eve sat at the table with Mary, eating bread and cheese and ham. Daisy plumped down beside them, a much more satisfied person than the one who had last seen the children. "Did you enjoy your visit to the stables?" Little girls didn't need to be writing numbers and letters all day. They should be outside building forts, riding imaginary horses, making snares to catch rabbits, or even building castles in the air, all of which she had done at their age.

"We gave apples to the horses," Dawn said, not meeting her gaze.

"Is that all?"

Both girls nodded.

"You didn't pat them or have a ride?"

Two heads shook. Daisy glanced at Mary, who shrugged. "I leave them to do as they please in the stables as long as they don't get dirty."

"What do you do when you go?"

Mary stared at her plate.

"She talks to the grooms."

"Only one groom," Mary said in a panicked tone, her eyes wide with outrage. "We're courting."

"How wonderful." Daisy aimed a grin at the servant. "I hope he is young and handsome."

"He is handsome," Dawn said, thoughtfully. "He has yellow hair like mine. But he's old."

"He's twenty-four." Mary frowned at the girls. "I thought we was keeping him a secret."

"Not from Miss Daisy. She is a nursery person like us."

"Exactly. If it is a nursery secret I am bound by oath not to tell." Daisy suspected as much from Mary, or not quite as much as 'courting.' She suspected flirting, but was pleased for the maid. "What is planned for the rest of the day?"

Eve tugged Dawn's sleeve.

Dawn said, "We could draw if you like." Her voice petered off into a placating smile.

"Let's do that until we think of something better." Knowing neither was particularly interested in drawing, Daisy rose to her feet. Mary brushed the crumbs from the table.

The art lesson went quite well. Both girls managed a stick-person shape, with a large round head and dots in the centre. Dawn added a smile, which Eve painstakingly copied. Then, they began to put marks on each other's pages, and squeal with laughter. Knowing drawing would go no farther today, Daisy eventually said, "I wonder if anyone is interested in having a story read to them?"

Eve nodded enthusiastically. Dawn watched Daisy's face.

"Do we have story books here?"

Mary, who was sorting through the children's laundry in the bedroom, stood in the doorway. "The Earl said we could use his library." She sighed, and her shoulders drooped. "But I don't read very well, Miss Gerard."

Daisy nodded, now understanding why the girls weren't interested in reading and writing. She'd loved both, but she'd had a real teacher, not a semi-literate nursery maid. Not finding in herself any interest in teaching the alphabet, she decided to fill their active little minds with stories instead. Books contained many ideas, which would help to banish the monsters in their heads. "Tell me where the library is and I will try to find something suitable." A good collection of books was imperative for children.

Given vague directions to follow, she took galloping

steps down the wide staircase, and stopped short at the bottom. The dining and drawings rooms were situated on the left, which possibly meant the library was on the right. If not, she would find out soon enough. She hurried down a passage with closed doors, and no hint as to what might be behind. When she reached the end, she opened the door to a storeroom. The next on the way back seemed to be some sort of filing room. The third, which had been the first coming from the other way, was a large library. Books had been planted thickly on the lower shelves and had seeded onto those higher. Without a catalogue, she would take a lifetime to find one suitable to read to the children.

"Good afternoon."

She turned. Lord Pretty Face stood in the doorway, his broad shoulders and easy posture giving him an athletic silhouette. "Good afternoon, my lord. I was looking for a story suitable to read to the children."

He nodded and turned to leave.

"But I won't be able to find one without going through them all," she said in a resigned voice, wishing he would offer to stay and help her. Sitting on her haunches in this room for what might be an hour or more, trying to find a story suitable to read to a child, would certainly try her patience. If she had been her sister, Cordelia, she would have blinked prettily and faked helplessness, and he would have been more than pleased to help. However, Daisy wasn't tiny and sweet, nor willing to be seen as helpless. "Could you point me in the right direction?"

He shook his head and offered her a supercilious tilt of his eyebrows.

She nodded curtly and turned her back on him. The

man was a boor and a dolt. Beginning at a waist-high shelf, she pulled books out, read titles, and slid them back. After a time span she estimated to be half her life, and a bout of sneezing, she gave up and marched outside. She knew exactly where to find the best children's stories in the whole world, and she could walk home and be back in less than an hour. In fact, if she ignored the pathways, she could possibly reach her destination far sooner.

After grabbing a hat, she hurried through the back garden and across the fields, using the spire of the local church to guide her toward the village. Deftly avoiding two curious calves, cowpats, prickly thistles, and the odd disguised rock, she made her way through the pastures, over styles, under fences, through hedges, and along newly discovered, hidden paths. A gentle breeze played with her hair as she walked, and she realised that she had lost her hat. Not wanting to waste time retracing her steps to look, she decided that no one of note would see her. She didn't care at all if any did. After trudging along a narrow cobbled lane, she entered the main street of the local village.

Walking always elevated her mood. The sun shone and only a few puffy clouds decorated the sky. Despite the lovely weather, she hadn't realised how dispirited she would feel about being left with strangers. Her pleas to be allowed to stay at home, even promising not to budge had been ignored. She'd been shunted off to a mere acquaintance of her mother's—though most people fitted into that category. Her mother had the world twisted around her little finger. However, she hadn't noted that her co-operative second daughter hadn't made a single promise about staying at Ashford House. If she wanted to, she could simply run away, or move back home, except not today because she was compelled to find at least one story book for the girls.

Being well known in the village, she nodded to the red-faced butcher whose open-fronted shop faced the town square. He stood in front of his butchered carcasses speaking to the grocer, who held a bag of apples in his hands. The flower lady, whose cart Daisy had often patronised, smiled at her, but glanced at her hatless head. Immediately conscious of being casually dressed, she turned and began to scurry.

The traffic was slow, only a few carts and pedestrians. The less people she needed to greet, the faster she could move along. She crossed the road in front of a wagon loaded with fresh cut logs. Clopping hooves resounded on the road behind her and then the rattling creak of harnesses as the horses drew closer. "Miss Gerard?" she heard from behind.

She turned. Lord Ashford sat on the high perch of a very stylish yellow curricle. Her heart began to patter. Surely he hadn't been sent off after her? She swallowed. "I'm going to fetch a book for the girls," she said in a horribly nervous voice. If he snatched her up and took her back, the villagers would gossip about her even more, which was the last thing she needed, when she wasn't doing anything at all outrageous.

He nodded, but he tied his reins to his brake, his expression deadly.

"Honestly," she said in a rather squeaky voice. He appeared to be about to step down and grab her. "I'm going home to find one."

His eyebrows high, he spread out a hand, indicating the seat beside him in the curricle.

She stared at him. "It's not worth the trouble. I am only five minutes walk away from home."

He stared, his gaze fixed on hers.

She would have backed away if she hadn't recognised the expression on his face had changed to steely determination. "Oh, well, if you insist, but it's really not worth your while."

His face hardened and he settled back into his seat, waiting while she hefted herself up the high step and into his conveyance. "Do you know the way, my lord?"

He blew a loud sigh and the curricle moved off, the horses urged into a smart trot.

She might have admired his handling of the reins if she thought this meeting was accidental. However, her insides twisted with annoyance. He was treating her like his prisoner. She was sure her mother wouldn't have said she needed to be watched. Or, at least not to a virtual stranger. Apparently he did know the way, although her father's estate was off the main road and not clearly visible to all and sundry. Within a few minutes, Lord Ashford pulled up his vehicle in the carriage drive in front of her family's greystone manor house, and glanced at her.

Stuttle, the stable-master, came hurrying from the coach house.

"Oh, it's you, Miss Daisy. I thought we had a visitor."

"I'm here to collect a few books, Stuttle. I can walk back, my lord. I don't want to keep you waiting."

The interfering pest tied his reins to the brake. Stuttle stood watching while Lord Ashford climbed down and assisted her, escorting her into the house as if she had asked for his annoying supervision.

Since she couldn't outpace him, she walked through the by-now-open main door and into the hallway. "The morning parlour is to the right. My bedroom is upstairs. I hope you don't mean to chase me there, too."

His sigh this time lowered his magnificent shoulders. The expression on his face looked watchful.

"Perhaps my lord would appreciate a glass of Madeira," said the nosy butler, upon entering the hallway.

She didn't hear the rest. Flustered and cross, she raced up the stairs and into the old nursery. Without looking, she grabbed a bunch of books and raced back down the stairs. "Done," she said to Lord Ashford who hadn't even had time to see his drink brought to him. "I would have been just as fast without you." She raised her chin.

"I am naught but a bee in the honey of your life," he said in a snark-laden undertone.

She stared at him, wondering if he was insane, but tiny relaxation of his mouth caught her attention. Not about to let him patronise her, she said, "Exactly." And she flounced back to his curricle.

She didn't speak to him on the way back and she used her coolest tone to thank him for his help.

Ashford, of course, knew he had no right to detain Miss Gerard against her will. The autocratic way he had handled her rather pleased him. Lordly, that's what he had been. He must have assumed his autocracy with his new title.

Normally, he was considered mild-mannered and easy going.

He sighed. Apparently, rather than having two small children to look after, he now had three, though the last was far more dangerous than the first two, who could be melted by kittens. The attitude of the third had him guessing why she had been banished to the country. The girl was a moppet, an elegant young lady one moment, and the next an infuriated racing hound, all legs, all snaps, and no sense. He had the same urge to gather her into his arms as the little girls inspired in him, but all three fully intended to guard themselves until they thought they could trust him.

He watched her flurry into the house with her bundle of books, and sighed, wondering why he didn't miss being in town. In his previous life, he had been a gentleman of leisure. His days were filled with entertainments, from gambling in the lowest dives and the racetrack, as well as boxing matches. By night, he filed with his friends into supper rooms and ballrooms in the never-ending search for a wealthy bride. He no longer needed wealth nor a bride. He was, in fact, finally free of his everyday drudge and now had a life filled with tasks.

However, even his mother didn't assume he could handle his new duties. He was, in fact, the only person who thought he was meant for exactly the role he had assumed, a guardian of a big estate much in need of nurturing, as was his mother, Dawn, and Eve, and possibly Miss Deadly Daisy. The latter three could be shunted off sooner or later.

"Shall I rub down the horses, sir?"

He nodded at the stable boy and stepped off the curricle, glad he had spotted Miss Daisy's dowdy hat in the fields. If she had planned to run away, her first attempt had been thwarted, but if she tried again, he really had no authority to make her stay. Perhaps, under his mother's calm guidance she would learn to relax and not see monsters in every corner, as the children did.

When he had first met them, they had refused to sleep in their own beds. Instead they made nests on the floor and stayed together for comfort. He had no way of discovering what had frightened them, as his second cousin had died and Ashford's inherited staff had mainly been dismissed in favour of him using his old servants who knew his ways.

Miss Deadly had mentioned that the children spoke of monsters. He didn't doubt that their world had been set on end. Their father had died at the battle of Waterloo. No more than a year later, their mother disappeared. Possibly, the responsibility of bringing up two tiny girls alone had been too much for her. Her maid had them taken to their nearest paternal relative, Ashford's second cousin, their grandfather, to bring up in the Cotswalds. Rod had inherited them with this house. Their lives had been disrupted every year. No wonder they saw monsters everywhere.

His mother had wanted to help, but she saw herself as too old to be a substitute mother. She advised him to marry as soon as possible, but how could he saddle what he expected would be a young lady with two children? Their lives had been disrupted enough. He saw no point in going to London this year. Best he got on with putting the estate to rights, and helping the children to accustom themselves to a new life.

"That was very kind of you to take Daisy for a nice drive." His mother moved into view, wafting into his study again. He must remember to keep the door locked when he wanted to work.

"She wanted a few books from her house."

"Don't we have books here, dear?"

"Apparently they haven't been catalogued. She couldn't find what she needed here."

"What did she need here?"

"I have no idea, mother. No doubt she would be willing to discuss the matter with you."

"Hint taken." She turned.

A man with a perfect mother didn't need a wife anyway. He consoled himself with that thought, though the presence of Daisy so close beside him still remained: her very feminine, outraged virginal presence. He didn't want to dwell on the hint of cleavage, the bright hair that hung untidily about her face, and the soft sulky mouth. That mouth appealed to him, he, who normally only ever noticed the womanly attributes. "Do you like Jonquil Beeby?" he asked as his mother reached the doorway.

"Of course, dear. Our families have been friendly for years. Why do you ask?"

"Would you like her for a daughter-in-law?"

"If you have your heart set on her, of course I will welcome her. But I thought she wanted Jeremy Hastings."

"All the young ladies want Jeremy. He would bless me if I took one off his trail."

His mother eyed him narrowly. "I suspect she wouldn't be too hard to divert. She would be well over twenty now and still on the shelf."

He concentrated on his fingernails, wondering if they

needed a clipping. "I don't want someone too young. I have the girls now."

"Sometimes, Ash, I want to shake you." She left.

He suspected many people wanted to shake him. On occasion, he wanted to shake himself. He never could quite bring himself to the point of appreciating the young ladies he met, year after year, looking for suitable husbands. The most suitable husbands had money and titles. Until this year, he had neither, and suddenly this year he was eligible. He could almost take his pick, but if he hadn't been good enough for a young lady last year, he was quite determined not be desperate enough this year.

Which could possibly explain why he had noticed too many of Miss Daisy Gerard's charms. She hadn't, and wouldn't throw out a single lure to him. At this stage, he didn't know why, but the reason would be related to her stay here and would definitely concern another man who clearly must be an unsuitable alliance.

He noticed more of her charms before dinner. She wore a blue satin gown with a blue overlay, frilled around the neck and the hem. "Do you always wear blue?" he asked, realising he had asked one of those questions he had in his head that he shouldn't have expressed. When he had been a stutterer he had hundreds of questions he never aired, but these days without the stutter, the paralysation of his tongue had eased a little.

She threw a quick glance at him. "I do this year."

"So you do," he said in mock surprise. "Does the date have some significance?"

"Ask my mother. She decides on the colours I wear. Last

year I wore pink, to match my fury about not having my season in London."

He laughed, appreciating her quick humour. "What colour would you wear if you could choose?"

"I'm rather attracted to any of the secondary colours." When he apparently appeared not to know what she meant, she added, "Orange, purple, green."

"I would like pink, Miss Daisy," Dawn said, tugging on her gown to get her attention.

"What colour would you like, Eve?" she said as quick as wink and clearly taking Eve by surprise.

"P-p-p-purple."

She didn't turn a hair either at the stutter or the fact that as far as Ashford knew, that was the first word Eve had ever uttered.

"Then I imagine that Lord Ashford will organise that each of you have an apron in your favourite colour." She pulled Eve to her and gave her a hug, extending her other arm to Dawn who moved into the embrace too.

Lord Ashford tried to swallow the lump in his throat caused by Eve's stutter. He couldn't meet the gaze of anyone at the moment while he prayed that no one mentioned the impediment. No one did.

After the children had gone up to bed and the three adults sat down to eat, he said to Daisy, "Has Eve spoken to you before?"

"No. Thank you for not saying anything about her stutter. I thought she must have a had a reason to use a spokesperson." She glanced at him and his mother, the expression in her eyes a plea.

He nodded and passed a silent glance at his mother.

His mother smiled at Daisy. "Best not to make anything of it. It will pass in time. What a relief to hear her speak. I must have the sewing maid to make up those aprons tomorrow. Her first word must be celebrated."

Daisy arrived in the nursery behind the breakfast tray. Dawn and Eve sat at the table, washed and dressed, hair carefully brushed back and tied with a ribbon. Smithson was also dressed, her hair in a severe knot at the top of her head.

"Well done," Daisy said to the girls and Smithson. "You all look lovely. I see you have managed without me. I'll leave you all to eat and visit the stables, and I'll be back later to read a story to anyone who wants to hear a story."

Eve smiled. Dawn said, "We want to hear a story about kittens."

"It so happens that I have one of those in my room. See you soon, my dears." She spun on her heel and hurried off to the breakfast parlour, knowing she was a little late. Since she had been told she could help Mrs. Toddleton with her entertaining, she had been a little more reconciled to being here. She had seen her mother entertain for years, and knew exactly, or somewhere close to exactly, how to manage. Lists first. Worrying second. Changing lists, third. Asking the opinions of others, fourth.

"Good morning," she said as she paced into the light filled room. "I'm on time, I hope."

"Breakfast is flexible." Lord Ashford didn't glance at her.

Boor. She smiled at Mrs. Toddleton who smiled back. "Good morning, Daisy. How nice to see a bright and fresh face in the morning."

Daisy sympathized. If she had to be in Lord Ashford's judgemental company every morning, she would be delighted to see someone else in the morning, too. "It's nice for me to see civilized people early in the morning. Mainly I only see my sister, Alice. She is sixteen and still a great pest. Oh, scrambled eggs," she said, noting the Earl's plate. "My favourite."

Lord Ashford nodded at the footman who brought over a covered dish and served her.

"It would be nice if the girls could have eggs sometimes, too."

"Don't they?" Mrs. Toddleton looked surprised.

"They have porridge and fruit because they eat early, but you eat early, too."

Lord Ashford directed his attention to his plate. "Are you criticising my decision to let them eat their meals in the nursery?" he said in a severe undertone.

Daisy raised her chin. "I'm simply making an observation."

His eyes met hers. "As soon as they are ready, they will be invited to eat with us. At this stage, they're still not conversant with knives and forks. Perhaps you could volunteer yourself to teach them?" The last he said with arrogantly lifted eyebrows.

"Will you have time this morning to help me, too, Daisy?" Mrs. Toddleton used a peaceful tone.

Daisy turned to her. "I was composing a list of names in my head last night for your supper dance. Perhaps Lord

Ashford would be kind enough to escort us to the assembly rooms on Tuesday night?" She tried to imitate his detached tone, but knew she sounded chastened, despite not feeling that way at all. Instead she seethed. She didn't care who ate with whom, and the sooner she left this annoying man's house, the happier she would be. "That way, you can meet a few prospective guests first."

"I would be delighted, Miss Gerard," the gentleman said, his gaze sideways, apparently not intending to glance at her face. "I paid my subscription a few months ago, but I haven't yet attended a function. Will it be a musical evening?"

"It's a dancing evening. The musical evenings are once a month on Thursday nights."

"How lucky we are to have a guest who knows all about these things." Lord Ashford signalled to the footman with an uplifted finger that he wanted his teacup refilled. "I'm sure you can introduce my mother to the local gentry, too."

"I'm surprised they haven't been calling."

Mrs. Toddleton lowered her gaze. "A few have left cards."

"Whom have you called upon?" Daisy glanced at the lady.

"Your mother. The Burtons. Many left cards but I was waiting for Ash to have time to call with me." She looked embarrassed, as well she might. Not visiting people who had left cards would appear to be rather arrogant.

"Shall I go through the cards that were left and sort out who would be the best people to visit first? Some of the neighbours know all the gossip and can save you a deal of time. I have my favourites, of course, and you might not agree with my choices. In any event, you will meet almost everyone at the assembly."

"You are a dear girl. I'm so glad you came to stay." The pink on Mrs. Toddington's cheeks had softened.

Daisy's eyes widened. "I'm almost sure I am glad, too." She grinned. "Because almost no one calls me a dear girl."

Lord Ashford eyed her sideways, but managed not to say a word.

"Don't you realise what a help you have been to us already? Neither my son or I knew what to do about the girls, and you already have their days organised."

"They don't need much. You have them downstairs before dinner and they talk to you, then. If they had a governess, I'm sure that wouldn't change, but I think they should have more time outside. I think that only happens once a day when they give their apple cores to the horses."

Lord Ashford said a single word. "Kittens."

"Kittens?"

"The children are not interested in the horses. They found five kittens in the stables."

"They told me they want stories about kittens and that's why I went home. I had a kitten story in my old nursery. I bought back other stories too."

"See? You really are a dear girl." Mrs Toddleton smiled at her.

Daisy stared a challenge at Lord Ashford but he didn't lift his gaze, the rotter. He should have had to grace to look abashed.

Instead, he remained totally disinterested in her.

Chapter Four

For the next few days, Daisy happily occupied herself introducing Mrs. Toddington to her most interesting neighbours. She had met those nearest, but not the best gossips—the shopkeepers who were more than useful, being the bearers of the most up-to-date village news. The little girls trotted along as well, though they tired more easily than the adults, a great blessing since that made the perfect excuse not to stay anywhere too long.

In awe of Mrs. Toddington's elegance, Daisy wished she had a larger allowance. The lady would have been a wonderful shopping partner, understanding so beautifully the styles that suited her. Not at all like Mama, who Daisy couldn't criticise, mainly because Mama didn't mind that she looked like a badly tied sack of potatoes topped with an enormous smile. The smile was more important to her, and she had stressed this often to Daisy when Daisy was being difficult. "Smile, Daisy."

Smile, Daisy. Nothing annoyed Daisy more than being

asked to smile, but she did smile today, for being with fashionably-dressed Mrs. Toddington and the girls was much more enjoyable than being with her annoying sisters. She stepped back into the carriage after she had boosted up Dawn and Eve.

"Where, next?" Mrs Toddington asked as Daisy settled her skirts. Today the lady wore an amber coloured gown with a delicious bonnet in cream, decorated with a bunch of amber flowers.

Daisy, of course, wore her usual dreary blue. "One last stop at the Middleton's house. Mrs. Middleton has no children and she would love to see ours." Daisy clapped a palm over her mouth. Lord Ashford's by-blows weren't hers, by any means. She hadn't seen the annoying lord since dinner last night, where he had spared her a mere glance. He was pretty enough to be a man who didn't like women. Perhaps he was. She sank comfortably into what her Mama would have called a nasty, judgemental smirk.

After arriving home in the late afternoon, she raced upstairs to change. Dinner would be served early. After the meal, she would attend the local assembly rooms with her host and hostess. Being forced to stay with the Ashford family had one *almost* redeeming feature. Smithson would be dressing her hair tonight. If Daisy ended up looking as fashionable as her hostess, she would be delighted to step onto the dance floor with anyone. Corrine would have said that she stepped into public far too often, regardless of how untidy her hair looked or whether her gown was patted nicely into place.

Even Daisy had to admit that she normally didn't pay enough attention to how she looked, but that would have to change if she wanted Jake to remember that he had promised to marry her when she grew up. Although she had been grown up for years, his memory had been inadequately jolted as yet.

Smithson brushed Daisy's hair up and made a loose knot. Then she teased out a few curls around Daisy's face. This was the simplest hairdo she'd ever had. For a moment she squinted critically, not sure if she wanted her fine hair to look quite so plain.

"Your hair is really pretty," Smithson said, examining Daisy's reflection in the mirror. "It's fine but thick, and the natural curl makes it easy to style."

Daisy kept staring, trying to judge, and finally decided that the hairstyle softened her face without begging to be noticed. "I am beginning to think this may be the right way for me to wear my hair."

Smithson smiled. "I've been wanting to fix your style since I first saw you, but you're always so busy that I can't catch you."

"Let me know the next time you want to catch me. I'm happy to stop if you can make me look pretty."

"You look pretty even when you don't bother. If you don't mind me saying, Miss, you have an interesting face."

Daisy gave herself her daft grin in the mirror. Having an interesting face wasn't quite as good as being beautiful, but looking interesting was a step up for her. After one last speculative glance at her hair, she rose and stepped into the gown that Smithson held, a fussy creation with a complicated pinch-pleated bodice and enormous puffed sleeves. The waistline sat under her bosom. Her skirts were rather sparse, as the latest fashion dictated. The whole thing made her look top heavy. Even though she would have preferred a plain bodice and tiny sleeves, Daisy didn't feel as overpowered by her gown as she usually did. After a 'thank you' to Smithson, she left for the dining room.

Mrs. Toddington looked stunning, wearing black with a dark pink lace overlay on the skirts, and a nice set of garnet earrings and necklace. Lord Ashford rose to his feet and seated Daisy, a resigned expression on his face. The man seemed to have no other expression other than boredom—except when he was speaking to the children. Then his face relaxed, which was about the only thing that kept her from despising him. His feelings for his daughters made her forgive every disdainful glance he cast her way. For reasons known only to himself, he had decided she was not worth tuppence. Her shoulders momentarily drooped.

She settled her skirts into the chair, hoping to placate him for this one single night, when she wanted to have dance partners gathered around her, the way Corinne always did.

However, when they reached the assembly rooms, he handed his mother out of the carriage first, and waited, tapping his foot with impatience while Daisy searched for her reticule. He didn't offer his hand. He grabbed her elbow and almost jerked her out. If he wanted to ruin her evening, he had made the perfect start by putting a frown on her face. She moved her elbow so quickly from his grasp that she almost tumbled off the step.

Accordingly, she marched ahead of him into the rooms, or tried to. He pulled her back to his mother, his face frozen. Of course she knew she had been ill-mannered by leading him, but he had begun the incivilities between them. She glared at him, but stayed beside Mrs. Toddleton while he acknowledged those who appeared to know him. He introduced his mother to the master of ceremonies and, in short, took over the evening in a high-handed way.

And as a member of his party did he ask her to dance, first? No. He waited for the lads she knew to come over and ask her. But at least they did and she couldn't say she didn't enjoy dancing, for she loved any form of physical exercise.

He danced with his mother once, but mainly spent the night settling her into conversations, leaving Daisy to have fun, for which she did feel some gratitude. His lurking presence would have prohibited the latest town gossip being told to her by her prospective partners. Not that she adored gossip, but the spicy bits could be useful. Although the last dance was a long cotillion, and she already had Andy Rutherford organised, Lord Ashford took her hand and joined the others on the dance floor, leaving poor Andy behind glancing after her.

When she finally had subdued her heated breathing, she noted Ashford's expertise on the floor, and the way every woman's eyes followed him. If they knew what an arrogant ass he was, they wouldn't be so enamoured of his looks. A stunning face was not everything. Being smart counted for more and, after having lived with him for a week, she doubted he had more than his looks to recommend him. His conversation lacked wit and he certainly wasn't verbose.

The last had never been a trait she adored in a man and she could forgive him for not boring her, at least. On the way back to his house, he didn't bore her. As usual, he didn't speak. She wanted to fill the silence, but when she came to think about people who talked others to death, she didn't want to be seen as one, and simply answered Mrs. Toddington's questions about her dance partners. "I've known them all forever," she admitted reluctantly.

She sighed. How much more interesting she would seem if she could hint that she had at least one suitor. But she didn't.

Ashford had enjoyed socialising with his neighbours. He had to admit he was rather impressed that his mother appeared to have met many more of them than he had expected. Most admitted to meeting her with Miss Gushing Gerard, meaning that the main distraction in his life had come in handy, at least.

Tonight, she had been tidied up. He could see why all the local lads liked her. She could be friendly and enthusiastic without flirting. She treated the males the same way she treated the females, with a happy smile and a bounce in her steps. She rather resembled a puppy, who had to identify everyone before settling down. He had never met anyone at all like her, but he was quite sure he didn't want to. Other than as a mother to his girls, he wasn't interested in women, bar one, whom he had lost last year to the former rake she had redeemed.

Unfortunately, Ashford didn't need redeeming. He had always watched his behaviour, not having been born to wealth or a high position. Perhaps if he had been less scrupulous, he wouldn't have lost the woman he loved. Although he'd later formed the intention of asking her stepsister to marry him, he had changed his mind. He couldn't follow Anna around forever, hoping for the dropped crumbs of her affection. Neither her sister nor him would find happiness that way. At least he had two little girls to worry about as a consolation prize.

He watched Miss Gerard stifle a yawn as he escorted her to the step of the waiting carriage. At last he had found something that exhausted her. Her bouncing energy wore a man out.

Had he been any one of his friends, after a night spent socialising with all and sundry in a village hall, he would spend his next few hours gambling or visiting certain available women, but he was tired of pursuing prizes he didn't need to win. Now that he had an extended family to support, he meant to learn all about how to turn a dismal holding into a thriving property.

At least he was now on good terms with the locals. His mother was his tipping point. He needed her as his hostess and tonight she had managed to be a support to him, instead of his faithful shadow. Little Miss Deadly Daisy had been *her* tipping point. Little Miss Daisy kept her amused. Instead of wanting to get rid of the wretch, he now didn't mind keeping her for a few more weeks.

In the morning he managed to clear his throat and say, "Good morning," to her, without the unmanly urge to whip away her chair as she began to sit. His resentment about having to chase her to get her back into his house still remained. He had wasted half a valuable day, and subsequently missed a discussion with a carter he needed for regular fodder deliveries for his cows, which in turn meant he had to waste more time following the man all over the district.

"Did you enjoy yourself last night, my lord?" Miss Gerard passed him a wary glance.

"Indeed. I was pleased to see my mother dancing in the cotillion. It's the first time she has been to an assembly since I was at Eton."

Miss Gerard's jaw dropped.

"I have been in mourning for many years, Daisy," his mother said after a quick frown at him. "I thought, perhaps, here where we are unknown, I could make a fresh start."

"In that case, I will take the place of my mother and make it my business to find a husband for you." Miss Gerard's face expressed pure mischief.

Ashford frowned at her.

"I am surely of an age where I can choose for myself," his mother said with a twinkle in her eye.

Miss Gerard grinned. "You can choose, but first we need to line up choices, though I can't help but think we would manage this far better in London." She batted her long eyelashes and raised a saintly gaze to Ashford.

"We?" Ashford faced her with questioning eyebrows.

"I'm a connoisseur of men. I have been watching my sister's progress for four years, now. I could have told her from the start who to choose, but she insists on aiming her sights at men who are wrong for her." She aimed her sights at her breakfast plate, and he saw her jaw muscles tighten.

"How do you assess a man's wrongness?"

"The best marriages seem to be between people who resemble each other in some way. My parents have similarities other than their short stature. They both have large expressive eyes. They both have short straight noses. They both laugh at the same time."

"Don't you think you are being rather superficial?" Ashford used his impartial tone, but her idea fascinated him. When he thought of the looks of every happy couple he knew, he realised they certainly had similarities, like height, features, senses of humour, and love for each other. He wanted a marriage containing the last two more than he wanted a marriage with the first two – that was, if he changed his mind and could raise the energy to look for a wife for himself and not simply a mother for the girls.

"Of course I don't. I have spent hours studying this." Her eyebrows lowered and she had adopted her Petulant Miss look again. "You may have more to occupy your life, but mine has been spent trying to …"

"What?"

"Nothing." She tore at a slice of toast with her teeth, her ferocious expression clearly aimed at him.

"A life spent trying to do *nothing* is quite admirable, Miss Gerard. Few of us can compete with that." He lowered his gaze to his plate, having been a master of doing nothing for the past twenty-eight years. However, now he was trying to do *something*, he wondered how he had lasted so long as an idle aristocrat searching for entertainment to fill the dreary emptiness of his existence.

"Men," she said in an exasperated voice. "You have choices. All women can do is marry."

"Many women have occupations, Miss Gerard."

"Many women have an education, Lord Ashford. Mine was in domestic duties and how to find a husband who could tolerate minor insurrections."

He fought not to smile, for he didn't intend to let down his guard. Instead he concentrated on his plate. This obstinate little Miss would take advantage of any male who gave her half a chance. The best way to deal with her was to cut her off before she grabbed a whole chance. He caught his mother's gaze. "What is your agenda for today?" he said, blatantly ignoring Miss Gerard's last statement.

Mother's glance rested indulgently on their house-guest. "Daisy and I are still on the throes of organising a dinner here. Now I have met a few more people, we should manage splendidly. Don't worry about us, dear."

Having duly been put in his place, Ashford finished his breakfast, concentrating on the various ways and means to have the roof fixed in the old wing without too much expense.

After a consultation with his roof tiler about his plans for the day, he listened to the butler's ideas about the reorganisation of the footmen's duties. From there, he heard about the lack of good maidservants from the house-keeper and her thoughts on the subject of the young females these days, 'witless, the lot of them,' and he retired to his study for an hour of worrying over his ledgers.

Apparently the hour expanded, because when a thumping noise came from farther down the passage, he looked up and saw that the morning sun had moved over the roof, and shadows had formed outside his window. He stretched his neck from side to side, noting the ache of concentration. Thump. Thump. Although he didn't mind the routine sounds of the servants going about their business, he couldn't imagine why bricks appeared to be thundering down on one of his polished floors. He waited for someone to explain. No one appeared.

Now curious, he rose to his feet and approached the doorway. He glanced from left to right. Nothing. Thump. Thump. Thump. The sound issued from the library. He strode to the doorway. A massive pile of books sat on the floor. Miss Gerard stood at the top of the ladder, her hair wild, tossing books off the shelves. "Stop," he called in a strident tone. "What is the meaning of this?"

She turned. The ladder tilted. She grabbed for a shelf and righted herself although he had hastily stepped forward to catch her. "Nothing," she said, her voice slightly panicky. "I'm tossing the books onto the floor and the exercise has no meaning other than to empty the shelves."

"My good woman—"

"I'm not a good woman. I'm a sweet child. Can't you see that I am helping you?"

He planted his fists on his hips and considered her words. "When did I express a need to have my books filed on the floor?"

"I pre-guessed you. I'm prone to mind-reading."

He suspected she was annoyed with his annoyance. "You must have a reason."

"Of course I do." She sounded cross. "No one comes into a library and throws the books on the floor without a good reason. My reason is to put other books up here instead."

"Did I ask you to?" He elevated his eyebrows and stared at her face.

"You would if you had ever tried to find a book to read here. The lower shelves are filled with religious sermons or stupid rubbish about plants or anything else you might not want to read."

"I *would* want to read religious sermons and stupid rubbish ..."

"You are not speaking the truth." Her eyebrows lowered enough to meet in the middle. "Can you see the wafting dust? That comes from the books I'm tossing onto the floor. The lower books are just as dusty. No one except me has been in here for the past hundred years."

"Do you always exaggerate?"

"Yes. Always." She tossed another two books down. One hit the toe of his boots.

He stepped back. "Well, stop exaggerating, and throwing. You'll damage the pages."

"I won't. These are the books I want to read and I'm dropping them flat, very carefully."

He didn't dare stoop to pick up one because he suspected she would 'accidentally' hit him on the head with the next few. "I don't know why I have to listen to this."

"You don't. Just leave, and in another day or two you will have a dust-free library and easily be able to find good reading matter. The last I can't promise because to date I haven't found much, but no one could fill all these shelves without accidentally having at least twenty or thirty good books to read."

"You can only say that because you didn't know the last two or three earls."

"I knew the last two. The last was a very nice gentleman."

"You were on good terms with him, eh?" The last earl was in his late seventies and his lack of patience with

Ashford's stutter kept him away, which explained why he now had so much catching up to do with his inheritance.

"I was. He told me I was a charming child."

"Which rather proves he didn't know you, doesn't it?" The next flying book missed his ear by an inch.

"Do I have your permission to keep working in your library," she said, her voice tight. "Or not?" She turned to face him.

He contemplated saying 'not' but having his books dusted properly appealed to him. "I'll give you three days and if you haven't finished and leave a mess for others to clean up, I'll have you horse-whipped."

She froze. Her eyes widened with disbelief. "My parents would kill you if you touched an inch of my skin."

"I would ask someone else to do the whipping." He held up palm to stop her further arguments. "Or I could modify the punishment ..." He turned his head aside and hissed an impatient sigh between his teeth. "Since I don't want to be killed by your parents, if you don't finish," he said, facing her, "I will think of some other way to punish you."

His last action before he left the room was to collect a book from the floor and replace it on the top shelf. He gave her a gaze of *do not touch this* and left the room to a stark silence, wondering how on earth he would see through his threat.

As soon as Ashford left the library, Daisy stopped to contemplate her behaviour. If she hadn't been so impatient with the dreadful books she could reach, she wouldn't have climbed the ladder. And if she hadn't been so unimpressed with the dust, she wouldn't have begun dropping the dirtiest onto the floor. She knew she shouldn't have messed up the library.

Finding a suitable book in Ashford's horribly disorganised shelves was an exercise in futility. She really wanted to go back home where she knew where every book sat in order, so that she could easily find something of interest. After having examined the bottom shelves and finding nothing other than religious sermons, she had lost her patience. Since she had another week or two in this house, she had decided that the least she could do was organise the library in her spare time. Religious sermons logically belonged on a top shelf out of reach of the unwary. Naturally, she couldn't reach the top shelf, and naturally she had grabbed the library ladder. And sneezed. Since nothing energised her more than having a good sneeze, she cleaned the top shelf, dusted the sermons, and placed the titles in alphabetical order. Then Ashford had raced in and had a tantrum. Arrogant ass.

When he had stormed out of the room, she examined the book he had replaced back on the top shelf, wondering what he didn't want to read. Being a book with pictures of flowers, she filed it lower down. The man hated flowers? Of course. He hated anything interesting. Muttering under her breath about his tastes, she cleaned the bottom shelf, scanning a few titles she had hurled to the floor.

Satisfied that she had treated the books the way they deserved to be treated, she began to move the books concerning landscaping. Title-reading turned out to be interesting. She found books on land management and moved them to waist height, though she didn't expect Lord Abysmal to take much notice, since he never read his books. By this time, her hair was full of dust and she had begun to wheeze. She decided to start cleaning up. None of the books were suitable for children but she found one about botanical specimens found in India and liked the drawings enough to grab up the book for the girls, who might appreciate the flower pictures.

On her way to the nursery, she heard her name called. She turned to the footman who held a letter in his white-gloved hand. "A letter for you, Miss."

She smiled, hoping Mama had written to say she could go to London. Her errand forgotten, she raced up the stairs. She whirled into her room, breaking the seal. Mama wafted on for a while. Right at the bottom of the letter she had added in a scribble that Jake was about to be betrothed. Daisy re-read that part three or four times, not believing the first time, not certain the second time, and aghast the third time. No mention of the lady's name appeared, but at least Corrine hadn't won his heart. Daisy's sank to her boots. Her chest thudded madly and her cheeks turned into agonised flares of heat.

She read the letter again. Staying here now would kill her. She had to go to London instantly. Her hands trembled, and her throat ached. She couldn't think clearly. Somehow, she needed to find transport. Without hesitation, she began to throw her clothes into her bag, not caring if any creased. She could lug her belongings through the fields and go back home where she could somehow convince the stable master to let her have at least the trap.

Or, she could leave everything here, and run home without a load to carry. If she did, she would be faster. Last time, Lord Abominable had seen her. This time she would need to be furtive. Therefore, she shouldn't take her bag.

She jammed her bonnet firmly on her head. For a moment she closed her eyes. She wouldn't let her heart shatter just yet, since she hadn't declared her love to Jake. Last time she had tried, the duchess, his sister-in-law had prevented her, which was why she was now here being supervised. Next time, no one would stop her. Jake had loved her forever and he didn't need to wait for her any longer.

She put her fingers on the handle of the door, closing her eyes for a moment of thought. Without a doubt, the stable master wouldn't let her drive herself to London, nor would he be convinced that she had to leave immediately. He of all people, knew better than to take her orders about transport. Papa had explained this to him years ago, when Daisy had wanted to go to see a balloon ascend into Farmer Brown's paddock. Papa had been outraged at the thought of a young lady chasing a balloon all over the district.

No one would believe her mother had said she should go to London, because Mama would first inform the household via correspondence.

Aside from that, Mrs. Toddington was holding her dinner party tomorrow. Although Daisy's presence wasn't essential, she knew her hostess would like her support. She eased out a long agonised breath. If she used her brain for an hour or two, she could work out a way to persuade her hostess that she shouldn't miss the London season now that she had a companion who would willingly support her.

First, she needed to imprint on Mrs. Toddington's mind that Daisy was her companion, which wouldn't be so hard if she mentioned the word quite a few times. Second, she somehow needed to imprint on Lord Ashford's mind that he adored her. Nothing spurred on a suitor more than a woman who had more than one man begging for her attention.

Chapter Five

D aisy made sure of being on her best behaviour during the dinner party. She didn't accept more than a drop of wine, and she directed her conversation into topics that would help Mrs. Toddington become familiar with the local events. As usual, Lord Annoying, his curly hair beautifully tousled, played the perfect male, being solicitous to his mother and only offering to the conversation the most thoughtful of his banal comments. Clearly, his guests thought he was wondrous. Daisy couldn't have disliked him more.

And then she did, because he offered her his perfect smile. Her dislike of him increased by the barrel-load. She managed a demure smile to answer him. His eyebrows lowered, which changed her smile into sheer amusement. He tilted his eyebrows, blinked with shock, and turned away.

"Do people honestly horsewhip other people these days?" she asked Mr. Grey, a short, stout landowner, on her right.

He seriously considered her question, because he would. He seriously considered every penny he made, and gossip said he still hadn't thought of a way to spend his fortune. "I haven't heard of a horsewhipping, other than someone whipping a horse in my entire lifetime."

"Some people think it's a la mode." She eyed Lord Ashford with a smile a hundred times smugger than his.

"If I heard of someone being horsewhipped, I would report him to the constabulary." Mr. Grey dropped his gaze to seriously consider the beef on his plate.

"I admire your gallantry, Mr. Grey."

Lord Ashford raised his gaze heavenward.

If she were a man, she would shove him out of a top story window. He consistently annoyed her. Even though he had made the threat, she hadn't believed for a single second that he would horsewhip her. He wouldn't dare because her father would kill him. However, she didn't have time to waste on thinking about revenge on Lord Atrocious. She had to be nice to him to get to London as soon as possible. To expedite the journey, Ashford needed to be convinced his mother would benefit before he would consider helping.

The next morning at breakfast, she began her first useful hint.

"You were a hit last night with the gentlemen, Mrs. Toddington. Mr. Grey could hardly keep his eyes off you." She held her breath, hoping Ashford's assessment of Mr. Grey didn't include him on his list for prospective step-fathers.

Lord Ashford's gaze lifted from his plate. "Good Lord. The man is twice her age."

Daisy adopted a virtuous tilt of her chin. "He wouldn't be more than ten years older than she. Do you like older men, Mrs. Toddington?"

Mrs. Toddington was still staring at Daisy. She blinked. "Did Mr. Grey stare at me?"

"Not only him but also Mr. Fox. Though he is a little prone to sermonising." Mr. Fox was a rarity in the county, being a bachelor, over forty, and not too ugly, despite being faint of heart. Not so many years ago, she had burst out from a hedge, thinking he was her younger sister, whom she meant to scare, and accidently caused him to drop his walking cane and trip over into a puddle.

"And you have assigned yourself the role of a match-maker?" Lord Ashford was beginning to sound annoyed.

Good. Quick rejections like that would work in Daisy's favour. "When she is stuck in the country for the season, she doesn't have too many choices." Daisy innocently tinkered with her spoon. "Most of the bachelors here have been snapped up."

"My mother is in no hurry." Although he tried to sound disinterested, his gaze said otherwise. He focused entirely on Daisy's lying mouth. "She has just begun to settle in here."

"Perhaps she would prefer to settle in her own place, instead." Daisy spoke in an undertone because she didn't dare raise her gaze, which she knew would hint at defiance.

"Thank you, my dears. You don't need to argue on my account. I don't expect to re-marry."

"Perhaps not marriage, but it never hurts to have dancing partners, or someone you can rely on to be your escort. In London, the gentlemen would be lining up to be your dancing partner."

"Women of my age—"

"Tosh. You should be on the ballroom floor if anyone should. If I looked like you, I would be on the first coach to London to enjoy the season."

"Daisy! You are positively lovely. If anyone should be in London for the season, you should."

Drawing out a mournful sigh, Daisy cast her gaze back onto the tablecloth. "Poor Mama can't supervise two daughters at the same time. I wish she could." She waited.

Mrs. Toddington reached out to pat Daisy's hand. "If I took you as my companion, we could both be in London." Then she turned to her son. "What do you think, Ashford?"

"Do you want to go?" His eyebrows appeared to be surprised.

"I can't help thinking that we ought to enjoy this season while we can. Your crops are ripening, even without your supervision. You can hand over the repairs to your manager, since you can't hurry-up anyone. All you seem to do is paperwork and I am sure you could also do that in London."

Lord Ashford's head tilted slightly, as if he was trying to shake a thought out of his pretty head. He melded his lips together and arranged his face into his usual bland expression. "The town house hasn't been opened. I've barely looked at the place."

"We can do more than look," Mrs. Toddington said thoughtfully. "We can kill two birds with one stone. We can be in London for the season, and we can give your town house a good spring clean if we take most of the house servants from here."

Daisy held her breath while Mrs. Toddington ran with the idea.

"We can send a few off tomorrow to stock the house with food before we arrive."

Ashford sat in silence. Apparently his brain didn't work as fast as hers or, more than likely, anyone's. While he continued mulling she tapped her foot with impatience. Finally, the earl said, "We'll need to let the Gerards know." He eyed his mother.

"I'll write note to Mama—"

He interrupted her to speak above her head to his mother. "I wish you had told me sooner that you would rather be in London."

"I wish I had known sooner. What shall we do with the girls?"

"Take them with us. Perhaps I can find a governess while we are in town."

The conversation began to flow exceptionally well without Daisy's input. She was amazed to hear the inarticulate earl relax into a light-hearted conversation with his mother. Perhaps he was a tiny bit human after all.

Her gaze followed back and forth while they organised the whole trip, detail by detail. Even Mama wouldn't quibble if her daughter was brought to London by the people with whom she had been lumbered. Apparently Daisy would only need to pack her bag, and her greatest wish would be fulfilled. Her chest emptied with relief and her heart lightened considerably. Finally, she would be able to meet Jake again.

The next day, the earl took her back to her family home and waited while she chose her wardrobe for the London season. Unfortunately, since she hadn't officially been brought out, she didn't have any particularly nice gowns. All were dowdy and over elaborate, which couldn't be helped. Jake had never judged her by her clothes. He liked her because he liked Her, and always had. His temperament matched hers, cheerful, with undertones of cynicism. He understood her humour without an explanation, and he was never boring.

Plus, he was tall and handsome, and an acquisition to any young lady's debut. She couldn't wait to see him again, and make sure that whomever was supposedly his betrothed was put back in her place.

No female would ever have Jake unless she stepped over Daisy's cold, dead body.

Ashford found himself re-energised by the idea of returning to London. He hadn't for a moment suspected his mother might enjoy the season. She had never expressed a wish to be present, and normally heard all the latest gossip from him or her dowdy cronies. Of course, she hadn't seen the latter recently, having moved out of her former district. He suspected she would know few people in town, but the fact that she was willing to try showed that she was hoping to find a life of her own. He would dearly love to see her married when she had spent her life making sacrifices for him.

During the past few days, Miss Daisy had been suspiciously helpful. Having finished settling the library in the order of her preferences, books that bored her out of reach, and those she deemed readable placed centrally, she had made sure the room had been cleaned from top to bottom. He had heard her giving orders to his servants, purportedly from his mother, although he didn't bother to check. Countermanding her would have been pointless for, although he would never admit the fact to her, the library was now quite a pleasant room to visit. The leather chair sat under the morning light of the window, and featured as a comfortable reading spot. He suspected that the seats at the table had been arranged for the little girls rather than him, but the thought was sound. When they could read, they would enjoy settling at the book table.

The idea of going to town had caused them to clutch at each other in alarm. Dawn had been placated by her doll, who had apparently expressed a wish to be wherever Miss Daisy was. Eve had been placated by Dawn.

As they were being loaded into the carriage, he realised they hadn't been out of this house since they had first been delivered by a nursery maid two months previously. More than likely, they had worried about being sent away. He had explained they were taking a holiday with him and would come back when he did.

"When we reach London, you will be able to see the sights," Miss Daisy said to Dawn and Eve as he loaded them into the carriage a few days later. "We can run in the park and hide behind the trees. You will have great fun."

"Did you ever to hide in the park, Miss Daisy?" Dawn asked, settling into the back-facing corner seat.

Miss Daisy laughed, sitting beside her. "You should

meet my mother. She will tell you all the dreadful things I did when I was your age. But I'm not telling the naughty things. I will tell you one nice thing about being in London. I saw a puppeteer."

"What's a p-puppeteer?" Eve moved in and crawled onto Miss Daisy's knee.

"A person who can perform shows with dolls who can talk and dance, like real people."

If they thought they would see a puppeteer, they were in for a shake up. Ashford didn't know a single puppeteer, or where he would find one, and he wished Miss Daisy wouldn't keep finding impossible tasks for him to perform.

Fortunately, Eve began to nod off in the early afternoon. Ashford changed seats with Miss Daisy. Eve slept on her knee while Dawn gossiped with his mother about the conversations she had had with Beatrice, her doll, who appeared to have a disjointed neck. With the jolting of the carriage, the doll's head kept bouncing from one shoulder to the other. Dawn held Beatrice aloft, watching the trick with a critical eye. She wouldn't doubt that a puppeteer had dolls that could walk and talk, since hers clearly did.

Ashford leaned back, stretched out his legs, and closed his eyes. The sound of female voices blurred into mutterings. The clop of hooves and the regular swaying of the carriage became a haven of peace.

"Will we say I'm your companion when we go out, Mrs Toddington?" Miss Daisy's low voice no longer grated on him. He had come to appreciate her modulated tones. Of course, the spoilt brat words that came with her nice voice irritated him, but in the carriage while she thought he slept, she spoke a little more humbly than usual. She wasn't giving her opinion on matters that didn't concern her.

"I'm afraid people will laugh if we do," his mother said, gently. "The other way around would be more normal."

"I suppose most people want to be normal. I suppose I do, too. In that case, I will have to be your friend."

"You are my friend. You are the best friend I have ever had, but you are also of an age to be my daughter. Everyone knows that you are not my daughter. I suspect I will have to call you my guest."

"I'll love being with you," Miss Daisy said in a lowered voice. "You're so elegant. When you walk, you glide. I wish I could walk like you."

"I can teach you."

"Will you also teach me how to look fashionable?"

At this stage, Ashford didn't dare open his eyes.

"I think Smithson could help there."

"She has done wonders for my hair. I need the rest of me to look better too, because I have a special reason for wanting to be in town."

"A man, I suspect."

Ashford heard a deep sigh.

"I have waited this past three years for him to propose but he seems to think I'm too young. He doesn't appear to have counted the years the way I have. I want to remind him that he loves me. First, I have to make him see that I'm old enough to be his bride."

"We will think of a plan," his mother said in a confident voice. "This is exactly what I am meant for. I have spent years waiting to be useful and now I have found a way."

Ashford mentally collected his jaw from the carriage

floor. He had never heard this tone in his mother's voice before. He had never known she didn't feel useful. Apparently, he lived his life in a contented bubble, not expecting money to fall into his hands, not expecting to be a landowner, and not expecting to inherit anything. He had expected to marry a nice, quiet woman who would live within his means. This new version of his mother sounded revitalised. The little girls hadn't managed to stir a hair on her beautifully dressed head, but now the most annoying female in the world could have his mother for a click of her fingers.

Air hissed through his teeth. Since he couldn't horse-whip her, he probably would have to be nicer, though he suspected that ignoring her would be the nicest thing he could do for her.

"Is the young man suitable, my dear?"

"Of course. My parents adore him. We have all known him forever. He told me he would marry me when I grew up, and I have. I don't look like a school girl, do I?"

His mother gave a soft laugh. "You look like lovely young woman. How old are you, my dear?"

"Twenty, almost twenty-one."

"Oh." His mother sounded surprised. "I would have thought around eighteen."

Daisy made a sound like a groan. "It's the gowns I wear. I keep telling Mama they're too young for me, but she doesn't listen."

Ashford also mentally adjusted her age in his mind. He had thought she was younger, too. But since she was indeed a woman, he wouldn't make excuses for her bumptious behaviour. He would expect her to act her age but even so, twenty seemed so young. At twenty he had fallen in love with Anna Winters, and he couldn't fall out. He thought of her every single day. She was Daisy Gerard's polar opposite, being responsible, generous, thoughtful, amusing, and Anna.

He sat up with a gasp. A little girl had landed on him, her knee very close to a wary spot, and was tickling her doll's head under his chin. "Beatrice wants you to wake up. She needs the potty."

"Right now?" Miss Daisy interrupted, her eyes wide and questioning.

"Right now."

"Could you stop the carriage?" Her eyes met Ashford's.

"Surely a doll can wait for the posting house?"

"Beatrice is asking nicely for Dawn."

Praying that the child on his knee could hold on for another minute, he rapped on the roof. The thought of any little accidents horrified him. The carriage halted with a groan of the hinges and a jolt. Miss Daisy grabbed Dawn from his knee and pounded out of the carriage as soon as he opened the door. He exchanged glances with his mother. "Should we wake Eve?"

His mother settled back, smoothing Eve's hair. "You take her, dear. I'm sure Daisy will manage her if you pass her on."

"Why didn't we bring a nursery maid with us?"

"We did, but she left before us in the baggage coach."

He gingerly plucked Eve from his mother's knee. The sleepy child put her arms around his neck and snuggled her face under his chin. Carefully holding her, he stepped out of the carriage. Miss Daisy was assisting Dawn behind a bush. "I have Eve here, too, if you don't mind."

"I don't mind. My shoe is already wet. Just a moment more and I'll return Dawn to you."

The leaves rustled, the bush moved, and Dawn bounced out, as bright as a cherry, and grabbed his leg. He almost toppled but he managed to push Eve in the right direction, suppressing the cowardly idea of returning to the coach with Dawn, but he knew Miss Dreadful Daisy would give him her impatient sighs for hours if he didn't at least try to support her. After all, these were his girls for the time being and he couldn't shunt them off to others too often.

With a nod to Miss Deadly when the deeds were done, he walked behind the trio, back to the carriage, trying to appear quite nonchalant about the whole thing. Miss Daisy certainly was. Nothing appeared to daunt her, from managing his mother to dealing with small girls. However, he wasn't about to let her get out of hand. Although he thought about smiling at her, he decided not to. Letting his guard down would be dangerous. She already walked all over his mother. He wasn't about to let him do the same to him.

The journey ended just before the daylight. Fortunately, the Ashford townhouse had been prepared for their arrival. The nursery maid took the girls, who began to talk in excited voices about the trip and going to the park to see a puppeteer. He eyed Miss Daisy with resignation. "I'll leave it to you to find a puppeteer. I'm sure it's not beyond your powers."

She gave a superior smile. "If I can't, my mother can. Don't worry about that, my lord. The deed is as good as done." That said, she followed a maid up to her allotted bedroom.

He hoped she had been placed nowhere him. He certainly didn't want to see her in the morning, or at any other time of the day. Fortunately, all his friends would be somewhere or other in town. He could keep himself well amused without a problem. Perhaps he would have to escort his mother out, once or twice, but she would soon find people she knew to take his place. As for Miss Daisy, he hoped her mother would arrive and remove her from his household. Having her under his nose too long might make him see her in another light, and find the amusement his mother had found. Ashford didn't want to. He wanted to find a mother for his children, one he could leave to her own devices.

The nursery maid gathered up the girls. Ashford heard a clear explanation of Beatrice's neck problem and how much the doll liked the carriage ride. The words disappeared down the hall. He breathed a sigh of relief. The first problem, that of displacing the girls, seemed to be in hand. Miss Daisy followed the footman up the stairs, apparently prepared to settle into whichever room had been allotted her. "Where have you put our guest?"

"In the family wing. We're all there. Daisy is in the room next to mine, and the girls are at the end of the hallway."

"That sounds cosy." He tried to appear satisfied, but he would rather have Miss Daisy in the guest wing. He didn't want to be running into her at all times of the day.

"I'm beginning to think of our motley bunch as a family. Daisy was so good, wasn't she, during the trip? I have never managed little girls, as you know, being my only son. She treats the children more like her little sisters, which I can see they appreciate."

"That's her trick, is it?"

"It's no trick. She is the most natural young lady I have ever met. I think she is adorable."

"Apparently her mother doesn't share your opinion. She didn't want her in London, and now we have brought her here."

"It's bad of me, I know, but I simply couldn't resist. I want her to find happiness, and she was frantic about being here. This man of hers had better be worth the effort, that's all I can say."

"Are you telling me that we are here because that bumptious horror of a female wants to be here?"

His mother cast a thoughtful gaze at the floor. "I think the whole thing will work out well. Wait and see."

He didn't plan to wait to see anything about the wretched female. After a light meal was served, he left for his club.

Daisy slept well that night, knowing she was on the way to achieving her aim. With Mrs. Toddington's help, she would be remade into a young lady, whose taste and style would hopefully turn Jake's head. Mama would be pleased, Daisy would be thrilled, and Corinne's nose would be put out of joint—three birds with one stone, so to speak. Not that she held any grudge against Corinne, other than not wanting her to steal Jake, which she apparently hadn't done. Daisy honestly loved her sisters and would support them through thick and thin, but a little rivalry between sisters was natural, or at least in her family.

She dressed the next morning in her blue frilled walking gown. Last night she had discussed shopping with her hostess, both she and Mrs. Toddington agreeing that she shouldn't land herself on her mother too soon, being a surprise visitor. By now, Mama would know her darling daughter was in town, but Mama couldn't throw her plans in the air with a bare moment's notice.

In the meantime, Daisy planned to visit a few dress shops with her hostess. Her gown allowance had not yet been spent, for she had been imprisoned in the country house during the beginning of the season. She began to count herself lucky, for she would be shopping with a woman of taste, which would give her a better opportunity to shine.

Lord Annoying didn't appear at breakfast, which made the first meal of the day almost a celebration. The girls joined them. Although the table ended up a little messy, Daisy discovered that Mrs. Toddington had decided to take the shopping trip as soon as Daisy was ready.

When the girls were taken back to the nursery, Daisy jammed her bonnet on her head and joined Mrs. Toddington downstairs. Her hostess, wearing in a smart grey spencer over a grey and white flower-patterned gown, stared critically at her. She reached out and untied Daisy's ribbons, placing her straw hat more firmly and slightly tilted upward. "That looks better," she said. Her own hat had been decorated with a scarlet silk rose.

Daisy offered a gormless smile and shrugged. Anything

her hostess could do to improve her appearance was welcome. She tucked her hand under Mrs. Toddington's arm and bounced down the marble stairs onto the street. With a footman following to carry the hoped-for parcels, she walked in the sunshine towards Jermyn Street, where she could visit the linen drapers, dressmakers, and seamstresses. Being with a sophisticated older woman with style was nothing like being with her chatty mother, who charmed all the sellers, but could never quite decide on what her darling daughter ought to be wearing. Her darling daughter had six month's allowance to spend, a goodly amount of money she had been given in compensation for not having her season this year. She had saved her normal monthly allowance to spend on hats and trimmings in London. Thus far, she hadn't spent a penny.

"I have enough money to buy at least two gowns," she said as she passed the first dressmaker's shop. "If we can find one readymade."

"How delightful. I had no idea I would be shopping with an heiress. I'm used to managing on a very small budget. Together we should do well."

"If I run out of money, I can always use credit. In an emergency, Mama wouldn't mind."

"Let's hope we can manage without an emergency."

Daisy discovered that Mrs. Toddington was an astute shopper. She helped Daisy choose two readymade gowns that only needed trimming to be deemed particularly smart. One was in orange muslin, dotted with white. The other was a plain yellowish green. Each flattered her complexion, somehow making her pink skin paler although each was far less subtle than any other colour she had worn. "What should we use as trimming on the orange one?"

The dressmaker stood back and eyed her. "White, Miss. Anything else would call more attention to the gown than to your face. If we use this orange and white striped fabric as a piping around the sleeves and hem, you will look extremely eye-catching."

"Do I want to catch eyes?" Daisy asked Mrs. Toddington.

"You certainly do. White is refreshing with the brighter colours. Perhaps you could have a pale blue with the green. What do you think?"

Daisy thought nothing. She had never given a single thought to matching or contrasting colours. "I think I have enough money left to buy trimming for my best evening gown."

"Is that the blue one, dear, the one you wore for our dinner party?"

Daisy nodded.

Mrs. Toddington averted her gaze, slightly. "Do you think we could remove some of the frilling?"

Daisy wanted to leap in the air with joy, but she said in a happy voice, "I think that idea is wonderful." Poor Mama would have conniptions. She adored every single frill she'd had added on. "But it's still blue."

"Blue is a good colour to use as a background. Don't worry. When it's simpler, you'll soon see how nice you look in it."

Daisy blinked. And nodded. Mrs. Toddington could do no wrong, in her opinion. She bolstered that opinion after she had visited Bond Street, Cheapside, and Mayfair, for a couple of hats, and more trimmings.

Chapter Six

Ashford opened his eyes to a blurry daylight and a head on the pillow beside his. Finally, he focussed and managed to say, "What are you doing in my bed?"

His friend since their days together at Eton, Jake Everley, lay on his back snoring beside him. He stirred. His eyes shut more tightly. "Do I know you?"

Ashford's chin slumped against his chest. "How often do you crawl into the bed of a stranger?"

A pair of bright blue eyes slowly opened and squinted at Ashford. "What do you mean, your bed? Correct me if I am wrong, but isn't this my bedroom?"

Ashford closed his eyes and reopened them. "Oh, God. Of all the people I would choose to sleep with, you are at the bottom of my list."

"Be grateful, you cur. Any other friend would have left you wherever we were," he said in a morning-husky voice. "Where were we?"

"No idea." Ashford sat up and stared down. "I'm glad to see that you left me fully clothed."

"I am too, old chap. I think we must have been too drunk to make love."

Ashford managed a weak smile. Jake, the younger brother of the Duke of Huntsdale, resided with his brother in Mount Street. Therefore, Ashford had slept the night in a respectable household where he would be offered a meal, a good brushing down, and possibly no lecture before being sent home. The duchess, Cassia, understood men and accepted drunken fools when forced by circumstances. This was such a circumstance. He'd been too drunk last night to care where he slept.

He had been fortifying himself with wine while discussing his estate problems. After a while, since Jake was more irresponsible about his inheritance than Ashford ever meant to be, he had stopped talking and begun drinking more. He could remember at some stage leaving the club and going elsewhere. "Where were we drinking, last night?" He rubbed his head.

"Let's not worry about the finer details. At some stage we'll have to go downstairs. Prepare yourself." Fully dressed except for his shoes, dishevelled Jake rolled over and fell out of the bed, landing with a thud. After carefully rising to his feet, and checking his left elbow for any damage, he moved over to the doorway and rang for his valet who had apparently had his ear to the door. Within seconds, the disapproving sod was in the room, gazing at Ashford.

He bowed from the waist. "I expect you'll want a clean shirt and cravat, my lord."

"Very good of you to notice. Thank you, Pensbury." Ashford cast Everley a knowing smirk. "Do you think I can fit my shoulders into one of Everley's small shirts?"

The valet reared back with affront. He peered down his thin nose. "Mr. Everley has a fine set of shoulders, sir. You won't have a problem."

"He's setting you up, Pensbury. Ignore him and bring us a washbowl. Fresh clothes for me, and as little as possible for Ashford, who will leave soon after breakfast."

His head filled with a beating tom-tom drum, Ashbury accepted the hospitality, mumbling about the lack of sympathy he was receiving. Insulting words were returned by Everley, and the two ate a companionable breakfast, without being accosted by the duchess. After gulping down a fortifying ale, Ashford began to take his leave. Clearly in a better state than he, Everley leaned back in his chair and finally asked him why he had come to town.

"Is now the time to gossip?"

"I've given you my hospitality for more than twelve hours. The least you could do is be civil to me."

Ashford turned, trying to relieve the crick in his neck by moving his head from side to side. "My mother took it into her head that she ought to be here for the season. I have no doubt that her latest amusement convinced her."

Everley's eyebrows hit his hairline. "Your mother has a *lover*?"

Though his brain throbbed with each of his movements, Ashford managed to shake his head. "Not a lover, no. Though, she is looking to be married."

"Attractive woman, your mother. Who does she have in mind?"

"I expect her latest amusement has some sort of plan. She was quite determined to come with us to London to organise my mother."

"She? You are beginning to intrigue me. Who or what is her latest acquisition."

"The daughter of our nearest neighbours. You probably won't know her. She hasn't been brought out yet. I don't know what her mother will say when she sees her, but mine seems to be prepared with all sorts of arguments."

Everley rubbed his forehead. "Your nearest neighbour. Do you mean Sir Patrick Gerard?"

Ashbury nodded. "The second daughter was left with us as some sort of punishment, more to us than to her."

"Do you mean Daisy Gerard?"

"Miss Dastardly Daisy."

Everley threw his head back and guffawed. "You have found the perfect name for her. Daisy is a prime one. I have been thinking for the past two years that she ought to make her debut soon. Well, I'm delighted to hear you have her. I'll call on her this afternoon. She'll soon cheer me up."

"Certainly, if I don't let you into the library. She has a habit of throwing books at people and she might throw a pile at you."

Everley laughed again. "I imagine you annoyed her in some way. She doesn't suffer fools."

"And she had been quite clear that she thinks I am one."

"I don't know how you managed to get on her bad side, but I suspect she will tell me." The grin on Everley's face widened.

"Aren't you surprised that she was left with my mother and not brought to London with her sister?"

Everley shook his head. "I would never question the motives of her parents. They practically brought me up, you know. Daisy is a handful, no doubt, but that's her charm. As you can hear, I'm very fond of her."

"I wonder if Her Grace, your sister-in-law, would like to take her off our hands?"

"I thought you said your mother was besotted by her?"

"I wasn't thinking straight. My little girls also like her."

"Girls? Oh, yes, I remember. They were left to you with the house. Shady way of doing things, in my opinion. How would it be if we all left people with properties? The country would fall to pieces."

"It's not so bad. I rather like them."

"Cassia is holding a supper party here tonight. Perhaps you will join us with Daisy and your mother."

Ashford nodded. "As long as we receive an invitation from the duchess. Other than that, I won't land unannounced on your doorstep. You are too casual with your invitations. I can't have my ladies denied entrance."

"Daisy can bounce in here any time she likes. The butler will welcome her in, and possibly let you in too. Though if he speaks to my valet, the situation could change."

On that note, Ashford took his leave. Now he was even more curious about the reason Daisy Gerard had been left with him.

Daisy had been allotted the best guest-bedroom in Ashford's town house. He had the master-suite, and his mother had the bedroom that had once been allotted to the mistress of the house. The girls shared one, since they preferred staying together. The large room at the end of the hallway was used as a nursery, wherein a nursery maid slept. Daisy loved having a room on the same floor as her hosts. Not sleeping in the guest wing almost made her part of the family.

Although she had blessed her luck that Lord Annoying hadn't appeared at breakfast, she didn't realise he hadn't spent the first night in his enormous town house until she saw him arrive home in his evening dress just as she and Mrs. Toddington prepared to leave for a few hours.

Mama had to be visited before Daisy could swallow her guilt about being in London when her mother clearly had left her in the country as a punishment for being rash and foolish.

His mother accepted his tardiness with aplomb, although she eyed Daisy sideways. "A night on the town?" she asked Ashford with high eyebrows as he stood in the doorway. A smile lurked around her mouth.

"I met Everley. He had nothing better to do."

"Everley? Do you mean Jake?" Daisy raced over to him and clutched at his arm, gazing at him, breathlessly hoping he had news.

He glanced at her hand. "Is there another Everley I haven't heard of?"

"How would I know? Did he say who he was planning to marry?"

Ashford shook his head and flicked off her hold. "Do you imagine gentlemen discuss ladies with each other?"

"Not being a gentleman myself, I have no idea, but why wouldn't you? Ladies discuss gentlemen."

He brushed past her and headed for the stairs. She glanced at Mrs. Toddington, using her eyes as a query. Mrs. Toddington shook her head. When he was not within hearing distance, she whispered, "It's not a good idea to question gentlemen who have been out late. They accept everything you say as a criticism about the hours they keep. We'll hear soon enough. Town gossip travels fast."

Not fast enough for Daisy. She would have raced to Jake's brother's town house if she hadn't known that would be a disastrous mistake. The duchess would find her again and drag her home by the ear. Since Lord Ashford was a friend of Jake's, she wasn't quite sure about her plan to use Ashford as her decoy beau. She would need to be careful around him now, for she knew the man barely tolerated her.

Standing as still as a statue while she thought, she decided that from now on, she would act as if Lord Annoying was Lord Adorable. If she couldn't make him a follower of hers, she would pretend to be one of his.

But first she had to face up to her mother. She hoped that Mama would believe that racing to town hadn't been her plan, but her duty to her hostess. If Mama thought Lord Ashford was taking an interest in her, she would be rather more impressed. Therefore, she would subtly let her mother think so.

She breathed a sign of relief, now having decided on her plan of attack. "Is my bonnet on straight?" she asked Mrs. Toddington.

The lady smiled cheekily at her and redid her bow.

Ashford, with his mother and his house-guest, entered the echoing, marble-tiled hallway belonging to the duke of Huntsdale. A butler escorted them through to the drawing-room. By some mystical means known only to butlers, he caught the eye of the young blonde duchess, who hurried over. Ashford introduced her to his mother. Polite greetings were exchanged before the duchess turned to Daisy and smiled somewhat ruefully. "I thought we were not going to see you this season."

"So did Mama, but I am part of the Ashford household for the time being. As long as I don't annoy Corinne, Mama will tolerate my presence in town for the short season."

This was news to Ashford. He stared at her. Tonight she had been dressed by his mother's maid and looked quite tolerable. Her wild hair had been tamed into a high knot, from which hung a few spirals of curls. She wore a severe orange gown with an interesting braid arrangement around the neck and the short sleeves. In a word, she looked elegant. Her posture had always been perfect, and tonight he hoped her behaviour would match, not that any misbehaviour on her part would be his responsibility. The Huntsdales appeared to know her well. He assumed they knew she could be a pest.

Earlier in the day he had received a note from the duchess for what she called 'a small supper party.' Her idea of small didn't coexist in the same world as Ashford's. He would rather attend a large supper party where he might pass unnoticed. His wish had been granted. More than thirty people stood around the room, each involved in a conversation. Conversations were his downfall. He never knew when his stutter would reappear to embarrass him.

The duchess, being the sociable sort of person she was, took his mother under her wing, bearing her off to meet her own parents, a smartly dressed couple standing in the corner with another couple he recognised as being related to Huntsdale. He appreciated her help. Left to him, she could only be introduced to his peers and she had already met all of them, most as scrubby schoolboys. However, this meant he had been left to converse with Daisy.

"I think I know everyone here," she said as he moved her further onto the room. "You don't need to stay with me."

Her words translated into *go away*. He imagined if he didn't take the hint, she would accidentally step on his heel or his toe or bump his elbow when he reached for a glass, but the little pest aimed a demure smile at him, instead.

All afternoon she had been making him nervous. Her behaviour had been exemplary. She hadn't given him a single order, she hadn't sighed with exasperation, and she hadn't stared at him as though she could see a bird dropping on his shoulder.

As he was trying not to be amused by her new improved demeanour, he noticed Everley separating himself from the group around the supper table, the wide smile on his face aimed at Daisy. Ashford glanced down at her. Her expression told him more than she would want him to know. The ridiculous child was completely besotted by the charming flirt.

Although Ashford didn't particularly like her, she amused him, and he had the odd feeling that he ought to warn her. However, bearing in mind the level of besot she showed, nothing he could say would dull the worship glowing in her eyes. He moved her back by using his forearm in front of her. "Steady on," he said in a low voice. Too late. She pushed three steps forward and placed her two hands between Everley's.

Everley dropped a quick kiss on her cheek. "I thought I might not see you this season, Daisy. Your mother said you were indisposed. I'm glad to see you are looking well."

"I've recovered, thanks to Mrs. Toddington," she said in an unlikely sweet voice. The overpowering adoration on her face was a surprise to Ashford. He had thought she was a tough little nut, but apparently adoration softened her.

"I'm glad Ashford has finally let his charming mother leave the country. Let me take you around the room to greet all your old friends, Daisy. Though, I expect you know everyone, already."

"Of course, I do. We've had friends in common our whole lives."

"You don't mind me taking her from you, do you, Ashford?"

He didn't mind on one level, and he did mind on the other. The lower level, that of being pleased to be rid of the pest for a few hours, warred with the upper level of not wanting her to be hurt by Everley's casual charm. For a moment he stood and watched the couple mingle and then he joined his other single friends, John Temple and Jeremy Hastings. These two hopeless idiots knew every debutante and went to every ball during every season.

"Who is that female you arrived with?" Temple asked. His birth was respectable, but his income could do with a boosting.

"Miss Daisy Gerard, the daughter of a neighbour."

"Gerard?" Hastings, Delmore's younger brother, appeared mildly interested. He was considered a catch for his income alone, but he was also an easy-going, mild-mannered chap. "Would she be related to Corrine? Corrine was widowed a year or more ago, Temple, now I'm put in mind of her. If you want an introduction to a pretty young lady who has money enough to support your hoped-for lifestyle, she might do for you."

Ashford stared at Hastings. "You know the Gerard family?"

"I met Corrine, who is now Lady Standing, when she made her debut."

Apparently, everyone but Ashford knew the family. His friends began to discuss the pros and cons of marrying a moneyed widow, and the pros did fairly well. He was astonished to hear that a sister of Miss Gerard's appeared to be popular, but no one could guarantee that sisters would resemble each other in any way. The decision was made that Hastings would introduce Temple to the young Lady Standing.

The conversation progressed to the muddier waters of Everley's latest fancy, a married woman, by all accounts, and pleased to cuckold her husband. Gossip bored Ashford. He tactfully glanced around the room and caught the eye of the duke, who introduced him to a glass of good Madeira.

His mood restored, and his stutter in abeyance for the

time being, he began to circulate with Temple and Hastings, letting the most convivial of London's society know he would be available as a dancing partner for the next month or two. His new title was worth something, if not himself and his properties. Although he scanned the room for prospective brides, the Huntsdale's guest list for tonight contained only happy couples or close friends, making this event the perfect place for his mother to start her social life. If someone of her vintage took a fancy to her, she could enjoy the ball season while being Daisy's chaperone.

As for himself, his life had changed a little. With his mother as his hostess, more than likely he could spring for a small function or two, himself. His previous role during the season had been to find a wife. Since he had now decided to help find a husband for his mother, he made himself pleasant to people her age instead of gathering with his friends to discuss which horse to bet on, which gambling houses had the best odds, where the latest cock-fight would be held, or the latest boxing match. For the first time, he realised that was no longer interested in the same pursuits now that he had an estate to run and two girls to bring up. His life had changed from being deadly dull into being strangely interesting, if not a little fraught.

When he couldn't bear to see Daisy adoring every extravagant word that dripped from Everley's lips, he moved her out of his vicinity under the pretext that his mother needed her. One thing about the conniving miss was that she had no hesitation when asked to be obliging.

That night, he left the Huntsdale's town house at a reasonable hour with two excited females planning whom to call upon the next day, and which invitations to accept. Despite the success of the evening, he didn't sleep at all well. Daisy's bright eyes and happy face disturbed him. A charmer like Everley would never be caught by a woman who showed her feelings so clearly. She needed someone other than his mother to advise her on her tactics, or his mother would never be free to call her life her own.

Daisy slept like a submerged rock that night, despite the unfamiliar surroundings. She was back in her own world of supper parties, assemblies and, she hoped, balls. Mrs. Toddington had already been told she would receive morning callers today who would arrive with invitations to various functions. Her hostess had been a great hit with the older generation, which was all Daisy needed. Normally, she had her mother who knew everyone, and was invited to everything, not that Daisy had been asked to accompany her too often. However, she had certainly been out and about, and knew how to behave, having been schooled on how to grab a husband, more formally known as 'how to behave in polite society.'

She arose in a good mood, dressed herself, and hurried into the room the little girls shared. Squeals of joy met her and she was hugged hard enough to yell, 'ouch' which caused more merriment. Apparently, the maid who had attended them this morning had already washed Daisy's charges. "It's Betsy," Dawn told Daisy with a grin. "She has three younger sisters and a cat."

"I'm going to wear a p-p-p–p . . ."

Daisy waited for Eve to find her word.

"She's going to—"

Daisy held up her hand. "Eve will tell me when her words are ready."

"Pretty gown," Eve said in a rush.

"Which one?"

"Can I sh-sh-sh-show you?"

Daisy held out her hand. The girls' dresses were kept in a trunk in the small adjoining room. Eve led her, apparently having finished her speaking for the day.

"Last night I met the man I am going to marry," Daisy said to fill the silence as she shook out the gown.

Two pairs of eyes focussed on her. "Aren't you going to marry Uncle Ashford?" Dawn asked, her expression wary.

"I think he would want someone much older, don't you?"

"You're old. And he likes you."

Daisy tried not to answer with peals of laughter. The man detested her. And rightly so. She'd used her best bratty behaviour on him constantly for she very much enjoyed his reactions. She terrified the poor mama's boy and he had no idea what to do with a woman who didn't swoon at the sight of his gorgeous face.

Last night had been illuminating. Women of every age stood wide-eyed as they watched his progress around the room. He didn't care whom he impressed as long as he impressed every female. He didn't have to say a word to have ladies glancing at each other and making secret palpitations signals. His habit of staring straight into women's eyes was a trick more men ought to use, more men but not Jake. She didn't want anyone else looking at him.

Although she'd been subtle in her questioning, Jake said nothing about being betrothed. Surely if the story were true, he would tell her to be happy for him. Therefore, her mind was *almost* at ease. She hadn't been brave enough to ask him straight out. Ashford had had a long talk with him, and if Jake had plans to marry, he would surely know.

She dressed the girls and took them downstairs. Mrs. Toddington had decided they would eat an early meal in the breakfast room. Daisy applauded the idea of having them learn to eat sitting at a proper table. The nursery maid took over from there, having ordered plates of porridge and serves of fruit, the preferred meal of the children.

Daisy next entered the same room an hour later, dressed in a dark pink day gown, having piled her hair on the top of her head, trying to copy the style Smithson had shown her previously. Lord Ashford sat at the head of the table. Mrs. Toddington hadn't yet appeared. "Good morning, sir," she said in her best-behaved voice.

He looked as if he had an ancestor who had died from smiling. "Good morning."

While his inscrutable gaze rested on her face, she experienced the same lost moment in time that all those women last night had. When she began to breathe again, her cheeks tingled with heat. "Good morning. Oh, I already said that."

He lowered his head and looked up at her. His thick eyelashes softened his perfectly formed face, but for the first time she noticed his chiselled jaw line and the hard sinews of his neck. She watched him chew and swallow, fascinated by the grace of his movements. Finally she had to glance away. If he had a brain, he would be terrifying. "What are your plans for today?"

Her mind blanked. "Dress fittings first, and then shopping. We need to be at home for the callers this afternoon. I think your mother already has an invitation for a small gathering at Lady Mountford's place."

"What about you?"

"I will, of course, chaperone her."

"You're not planning on doing any gallivanting?"

"Not tonight. First we need to gather up all the invitations we can and then we can decide on which we think will be offering the most gallivanting."

He laughed. He leaned back and actually laughed. "Let me know which you decide on, and I will escort you."

"That won't be necessary."

"It's essential. I can't have you flirting with every man you meet."

"Why not?"

"I'm not sure you can handle men, yet."

"What would you know?"

"I've been a man my whole life."

She gazed at her plate long enough to manage to repress a most unladylike chortle. "Speaking of men ..."

"No."

"You don't know what I am about to say." She leaned back and crossed her arms.

"You are about to ask me a question about men."

"I'm not." She was.

"Good morning everyone." Mrs. Toddington walked into the room and waited while the footman pulled out her chair. Her grey and white gown was a study in elegance, and yet Daisy knew how little the lady spent on her gowns, compared to how much Daisy spent on hers. "Are you two bickering again?"

Daisy examined her fingernails. Lord Ashford said, "What do you mean by 'bickering?'"

"I think I'll give up here if I have to give a definition. What are your plans for today?" Mrs. Toddington aimed her indulgent glance at Daisy.

Daisy glanced at Ashford.

"Dress fittings, shopping, being home for callers, sitting with embroidery," he answered for her, eyeing her sideways.

"I didn't include embroidery." She raised his chin.

"What else would you do if you aren't doing anything else?"

She frowned at him. "I don't know about your mother, but I would like to practice draining a brandy bottle in under three seconds, the way you do."

He studied her expression. "I see I will have to keep you away from Everley in the future."

She was about to make a hot rejoinder when she noticed the hopeful expression on his face. "Tell me what my answer might be to that?"

Mrs. Toddington rose to her feet. "I think I will leave you two to battle to the end. Let me know who you decide is the winner." She left the room with an innocent expression on her face.

Daisy heaved a sigh. She'd wanted to learn how to be a sophisticated woman from Mrs. Toddington, and she thought she'd had her first lesson. Dropping her chin to her chest, she concentrated on her tapping fingers. Ashford had baited her and had successfully caught her on his hook. He had won this battle but she would win the next. No one deliberately annoyed Daisy Gerard without being truly sorry to have messed with her.

Plastering a superior smile on her face, she rose to her feet and left, determined not to let down her guard against Ashford again.

He didn't play fair. He used his gorgeous face to distract people into thinking he was a pushover.

Chapter Seven

N ow that Ashford had settled into his town house, he took his time to examine his new abode thoroughly.

After his entertaining breakfast, he started his explorations. The lower ground floor contained the kitchens, storage space, and the wine cellar. A box room and servants' quarters filled the next floor. He wandered around the second floor, which housed the large dining room, a formal sitting room, a smallish ballroom, and a music room. All needed an amount of refurbishment. He noted the peeling wallpaper in the ballroom and the scuffed wooden floors, and visualised how grand this room could be with a minimal amount of effort. The paper could be glued, the windows could be properly framed with curtains, the chandeliers could come down for a good washing, and the floors could be polished. He would set his two footmen onto the task.

As he reached the grand entrance at the top of the stairway, he bumped into Miss Gerard. "Spying are you?"

"Of course. Why wouldn't I?" She raised her belligerent chin.

Instead of continuing what would turn into another argument, he said, "I suppose you are like this because you come from large family."

"Like what?" Her pretty chin lifted higher.

"So easy to goad."

"I am n ..." Realising she would prove his point if she continued, she stopped and frowned. Her large, expressive eyes fixed on his. He tried and failed to discern the colour but the range sat somewhere between blue and green "My sister always expected to get in the last word, which meant that she made me feel stupid. I suppose at some time I decided that I also had an opinion that had a right to be heard."

"It does, Miss Gerard. But not on every single subject. You wear a person out with all your niggling. I would much prefer to be on your side than oppose you, amusing as it has been."

"Amusing?"

"Of course. I'm an only child. I didn't have the benefit of being howled down every time I spoke. Instead I had the attention of everyone when I tried." He decided to take his focus to the floor.

"I would have loved that."

He smiled. If she had everyone's attention because she stuttered, she would soon see why some people simply said as little as possible to get across their point. "Too late. You have to play with the cards you get." He turned and indicated the ballroom. "I am mulling about readying this room for a small function this season."

"It's a good size," she said after a moment's consideration. "You could hold a grand ball here."

"One day, perhaps, but this is my mother's first season since she met my father. I was thinking more along the lines of a supper dance."

"If you don't mind me using the royal 'we,' I think we could manage that between us."

"As my mother's social secretary, your advice is valued."

She glanced at him warily. "I'm not completely useless, you know."

"I'm sure you're not. I can use you at this very moment." He held out his hand to her. "Care to test the floor with me?"

"What do you mean?" She took a step back.

"A waltz around the room."

"I can't waltz." She glanced away.

He examined her expression, easily able to acquit her of being embarrassed, knowing she had enough front to advertise a draper's store. "Why."

"I haven't been allowed because I'm not officially out yet."

Her tone said this was a major irritant to her, and he sympathised. When she finally made her debut, she would be older than the others in her set. For a forward and smart young lady like her, this would make her season deadly dull, if not embarrassing. "Do you know the steps?"

"I have practiced with my sisters as my partner."

He needed no other encouragement to look into her eyes and frown menacingly. "All you need to do is count to three, which I presume you can do. Music will not be required."

For a moment she appeared to want to argue, but she finally nodded and took his hand. He stared straight into her eyes, stepped in front of her, and put his other hand on the flat of her back. "Put your feet together and I will begin the count. Stare over my right shoulder. Ready?"

She nodded and stared behind him.

"Step back with your right foot," he said walking into her. "Step to the left," he said with the next step, and she trod on his toe. "Pause," he said in a pained voice, and then "Forward, right, close." She managed to follow, although a little clumsily, but he kept up the count and soon she had adopted his rhythm. He kept her on repeat and then began to circle around the room with her. Apart from being trampled on a few times, and having her numb the fingers on his right hand, he coped rather well. He'd spent six or more seasons being everyone's partner, including, at times, women he was more than pleased to hold in his arms. "I'm going to call you Daisy from now on."

"I'm going to call you *my lord* from now on."

"Isn't that what you have been calling me?"

The little horror grinned at him.

He frowned at her. "What have you been naming me in your mind?"

"I'm afraid that will remain my secret."

Although he was prone to stammering, he never combined that with being embarrassed, which meant he could maintain his cool expression as long as he didn't laugh. Today the mischievous smile she used seemed rather more companionable than her judgemental glances, and gave him the impression she had begun to like him. He had previously thought her eyes to be her best feature, but her constant cheeky insurrection had lightened his heart.

Although he hadn't been patient with her, or kind to her, she had remained his mother's and his girls' staunchest ally. She would be the last woman he would pair with Jake, who had no sense of responsibility whatsoever. Putting those two together would be like serving up sautéed lamb cutlets to a wolf—unnecessary.

He wouldn't stand in her way, of course, but he also wouldn't help. If she wanted handy hints about men, he would give her handy hints. None would be in the least useful to her.

When he thought her steps had become automatic, he stopped waltzing, and bowed to her. "I think we have now tested every floorboard. I'll set the housekeeper onto the job of refurbishing the room. It seems useable."

"The curtains would probably revive after a good beating," she said in a thoughtful voice.

"What did you want to ask me about men?"

"Nothing." Her stubborn chin lifted.

"Because I wouldn't want to be ungracious to my dancing partner, I'll tell you one thing. Men prefer a woman who can stand on her own feet, not ours." He glanced down at scuffed toes of his shoes. "We like independent women, who don't chase us, because we think we are the hunters."

She managed a few, a very few seconds of complete silence and then she made a face like a bull terrier, jaw jutted, teeth showing. "So, all men think alike, do they? In other words, you think all men are the same. I hope you don't think all women are the same, because we're not."

He clasped his hands behind his back and leaned down from the waist to frown straight into her eyes. Unfortunately, he forgot what he meant say to her. His mind completely blanked the moment he focussed on her mouth. She appeared not to have a word to say, which was so incredible that for no accountable reason, he kissed her. The shortest kiss in which he had ever been involved set his heart thundering in the same way his first kiss had all those years ago. He quickly straightened his back. "I d …" He stopped rather than to rushing into a series of 'di-di-di' that would finish with 'didn't mean to do that.' Over the years, he had learned to focus on alternative words rather than to keep trying to fix his pronunciation. "That was just an example of what some men do when a woman is alone with him."

"Well, you could have said so. You didn't need to give me an example." She stood with her back ramrod stiff, her face still, and her eyes as wide as full moons.

He folded his arms across his chest and adopted a noble stance. "I could have told you how to waltz, but instead I showed you. Showing is more effective than telling." Instead of being apologetic about the kiss, he stood until she lowered her gaze. While staring at the top of her head, he realised he'd had his first victory over her. Triumph flooded him. He hadn't left her at a loss during any former encounter.

"Now I only need to work out how to be alone with someone I want to kiss," she said, trying from her lower height to look down her nose at him. Having reverted to type, she turned around, swished her skirts, and strolled out of the room.

His chest deflated. His short moment of triumph had ended but he didn't mind at all. He had worked out how to momentarily confuse her. From now on, he would work on extending that moment. His life had begun to become interesting once more. Nothing suited him more than a challenge.

~

"Lord Ashford seems to think that the ballroom could be used for a supper dance," Daisy said to her hostess later on in the day. She still couldn't quite believe that

Ashford had accidentally kissed her. His accident may well have been an accident, unlike her 'accidents.' One thing she could be certain about—he had paid her back in kind. She should be outraged, but she wasn't. What he had done was adorable, although he hadn't meant his action that way. "He seems amenable to entertaining."

"Until he succeeded to the title, he had no more than two pennies to rub together, and he couldn't afford to hold even the smallest function. His father left him with a small income, and the country property that we lived on until last year. All the land had been sold off before he inherited." Mrs. Toddington lifted her hands. "My now deceased parents made sure that my own income was tied up in the funds, but they paid for his schooling. After they died and my brother inherited ..." She shrugged.

Daisy averted her gaze. She had an inheritance from a maternal aunt that would be settled on her when she turned twenty-one. Other than that, she had a reasonable gown allowance, which she was never supposed to exceed. She never had, not being more than a little interested in how she looked. "Although I don't like to be a person who mentions the obvious, but your son is ..." She eked out a breath. "If I am to be honest, Lord Ashford is strikingly handsome. He could probably have an heiress with a click of his fingers."

"I don't doubt that, but he has never shown the slightest interest in marrying for money. He fell in love years ago, and I don't think he has coped well with her marriage."

"Oh? He has a broken heart. That's why he is so contrary."

Mrs. Toddleton smiled. "Do you see him as contrary? He has a rather dry sense of humour. It takes a time to get used to him, but he doesn't have a bad thought about anyone. He is almost too perfect."

"As a matter of fact, that's exactly what I was thinking. He is kind to children, animals, and houseguests. But he never seems to be emotionally involved. He acts like one of life's onlookers."

Mrs. Toddleton stared at her as if she was trying to enter her mind. "I think you may be right. The girls are helping him no end. I rather think you are too."

"I'm not. I know I annoy him."

"But he seems to enjoy being annoyed by you. I love seeing the wheels of his mind turning. He has been too passive for far too long. He needs something other than chasing unneeded money to occupy his mind. Not every landowner needs to make a fortune in the first two years."

"I suspect that not having a fortune has spurred him on. Most of his friends are very well off."

"Most of his friends inherited money. None had to work out how to make money. They all follow in the footsteps of their fathers. Ashford's father was a man worth following because of his beautiful nature, but not necessarily an acquisitive one. Which begs the question. Who is the better man? The one who makes a fortune at the expense of depriving his family of his company, or vice versa?"

Daisy tapped her fingers on her chin. "Neither. Families need to be happy but they're never going to be happy if they're starving. I think the way to live is to combine both. But who am I to prose on? I have never had to earn a living, and don't expect that I ever will." She gazed down at her white, useless hands, for the first time realising what her mother went through day after day.

Mama had married into money, but she loved Papa. She also combined charitable works with living a good life herself. The duchess of Huntsdale was the same. This was the reason why the two, despite a disparity in age, got along so well. And Daisy did nothing but plot against her sisters and spend money, when she ought to have her mind on being kind rather than competitive. She lifted her gaze, knowing she could help Ashford if she chose, rather than hinder him. "Ashford wants to hold a supper dance. I would like to help, if I can."

"You will be great help. I haven't been in the social scene for so long that I have forgotten more about organising functions than I knew in the first place."

"It won't hurt to make up a guest list, but we ought to go out and about and meet more people. Not that I don't know almost everyone. My mother is a regular gadabout and she has made sure of that. However, I'm only her second daughter and although I know people, I don't have the ability to invite anyone I know anywhere. But you do because you are the mistress of this house. I think if we stick to the Huntsdales, we will gather moss on our stone."

"Perhaps you mean 'no' moss?"

"One or the other." Daisy shrugged away the question. "My mother won't be at the Huntsdales' often because she has to get rid of Corinne, and the Huntsdales' crowd the place with their friends. They're too interesting for Corinne. She likes boring people, and she would want a conservative husband."

"What sort of husband do you want?"

"A charming rogue."

Mrs. Toddington examined her face. "Of course you do."

"Would you call your son a charming rogue?"

Mrs. Toddington shook her head. "But I'm his mother. He isn't roguish with me. He's kind-hearted and support- ive. Who else would take two small children under his wing when he doesn't even have a wife to help him? Most people would shunt them off to an orphanage."

"He's not related to Dawn and Eve? I thought he said they were his cousins." Daisy hadn't believed a word of that from the beginning. The girls looked like him with curly hair and pretty faces like his.

"They could be the children of the last earl's daughter but we haven't traced the birth certificates yet. The earl, who is Ashford's second cousin, said they were hers, but we haven't been able to trace her."

Daisy listened carefully. Even the last earl's daughter couldn't inherit the property after he died because primo- geniture would cut her out, but Dawn and Eve should have some sort of inheritance coming to them if they indeed were related to the previous earl. Perhaps Ashford was hiding them away from the world while he spent their money. Anyone with his face and body would get away with being pure evil, as he had proven by kissing her.

She hadn't said a word and wouldn't. He would know that. He'd probably kissed half the women in England and left them blessing their luck. Well, she wouldn't be another one of his conquests, no matter how pleasant he pretended to be around her.

She straightened her back and sat forward in her chair. "We need a plan of attack." She was still thinking of Ashford kissing her, and the thought wouldn't leave. Her lips tingled, but worse, her mind kept racing back to the scene of the kiss. He hadn't warned her in any way, and she didn't know how anyone could kiss another person without appearing as though they might. He had gotten away with the kiss because he seemed like a man with no ulterior motive.

"For finding the mother of the girls?"

"No, for inviting people to our supper dance. We want interesting people, not young debutants on the hunt. So, I'll have to follow you around and see who shows interest in you."

"I would also want people Ashford's age, or he will be bored and leave. I suggest we find people with daughters past their first season. That should work for Ashford's friends too. Most aren't married, yet."

"What size function would you say is small?"

"No more than forty people."

Daisy nodded. Forty could be fifty, but she would see

who she could find that might be able to look past Jake and distract Ashford's attention. She didn't want him to kiss her again when she wasn't noticing.

Ashford spent the morning consulting with the housekeeper about the refurbishment of the ballroom. She wasn't the most organised woman he had ever met. In fact, since she had a hard time making a decision, he searched the attic rooms. He found exactly the chairs he wanted, racked up in one corner; old dining chairs, he suspected, but useful to set about in groups. A trio of maids took on the task of cleaning them up, polishing the windows, and scrubbing the walls. Old smoke from the candles in the two chandeliers had left yellowing stains. The floors would have to wait for another day or two.

Domestic matters not being his forte, he took himself off to find his cronies in the afternoon, the girls having been promised a trip to the park by Miss Daisy.

He'd meant to join Temple and Hastings in the evening, but he decided a family night would be more valuable for plotting the supper dance. The ladies would need a budget in the very least, but he wanted to check the guest list to make sure Daisy hadn't invited a pack of giggling debutants. He also wanted to make sure she hadn't invited the Delmores. The sight of Anna in love with her husband had become a never-ending source of heartache to him. He wanted her to be happy, but he didn't want to be tortured by her happiness too often, and especially in his own home. In crowds he could cope, but not in a small gathering.

After the girls had been brought downstairs to say their goodnights, he settled down to a good meal while the ladies discussed the food and the drinks for the supper dance. He didn't listen because he didn't care what anyone ate or drank. "Have you two settled who you want on my guest list, yet?"

His mother turned to him. Her eyebrows creased with concentration. "We'll want the families who have been kind to us, the Huntsdales, and of course, Daisy's family. You will want the Delmores, too."

While preparing an excuse in his mind for not inviting them, he pulled the tentative list he'd begun out of his jacket pocket. "I expect they'll be far too busy. Hastings says they're planning to leave town. We'll have him alone, without his brother and his sister-in-law. If Daisy has a few young friends, I have a few bachelors at the ready." His list showed three extra males.

"I wish we could think of a way not to have my sister."

"We have to have her," he said in a deliberately bored voice to Daisy. "I must meet this paragon of virtue."

Daisy stared at him as if he had just sprouted horns. "You don't even know her. But if you are inviting my mother ..."

"Are we inviting her mother?" He queried his mother with his gaze.

"Of course, dear. How could we not when we have borrowed her second daughter for the season?"

He adopted a look of concentration by blanking his face and staring at the opposite wall. "If we do, someone will have to watch Daisy. If her sister annoys her, she is liable to push her down the stairs."

"I've had twenty years with her, and I have never pushed her down the stairs." Daisy's indignant expression was a joy to see. "She tripped me once, and I was careful thereafter."

"How entertaining it must be to live with sisters. Bertie must be a happy chap to have experienced all the rivalry."

A superior smile half-closed her eyes. "It was a good experience for him. He is now happily married."

"Why do I always feel nervous when you smile?"

"You? Nervous? I am sure are plotting something ghastly like teaching me how to waltz with a man."

"Would that be ghastly?" his mother said, staring at him.

"Ask her."

"He only wanted to use me to test the floorboards." Daisy avoided looking at him.

"So, it wouldn't be ghastly if I had wanted to waltz with you?"

Daisy eyed him sideways, and then turned to his mother. "I'm sure you agree that waltzing with a man who didn't want to waltz with you is ghastly."

His mother's bland expression puzzled him. She caught his gaze and quickly averted her eyes. "It could be," she said in very careful voice.

He glanced at Daisy, who had begun to realise who she was criticising to whom. She blinked rapidly and put her hand on his mother's arm. "I was only joshing Lord Ashford. I love dancing with your son. He is a far better partner than my sister. She made me lead, and, of course I guided her into the piano. She tripped over the stool. I didn't push her, honestly. Going around in loops made me dizzy."

His mother laughed. "Forgive me, dear Daisy. I've never been more amused than when I hear you ragging my son. Everyone else treats him like a precious jewel."

He frowned and rose to his feet. "So, this is what comes from family meetings. Nothing. Each time I try, you two go into gossip mode and all my lists are ignored." Using his faked annoyance as an excuse, he left, but he hadn't been joking. Every time he tried to organise a mere two of the females who filled his house, he ended up being outnumbered by incidentals. Herding cats, might have been a more apt description. He went to his club where women were banned.

And ended up being bored for two whole hours. Drinking and discussing women of easy virtue no longer interested him. He had turned into a regular homebody, thinking about his household instead of his entertainments, and thinking of waltzing with Daisy instead of holding Anna in his arms.

When he had stopped reaching for love, a weird sort of contentment had found him at home.

Daisy realised that Ashford was starting to influence her too much. She was beginning to behave like a simpering fool, because he seemed to enjoy her nonsense. Who would have thought that misbehaving when she was told to behave would reap the reward of his laughter? Now all she wanted to do was entertain him more with her dysfunctional family stories.

Cornelia wasn't half as bad as Daisy depicted, and she really didn't fight back much. Instead she watched her older sister with a critical eye, judging her all the time. She didn't want to fail the way her sister had, marrying one man when she had always wanted another. Fortunately, her husband had died and she could now try for her true love, who also happened to be Daisy's, but Jake had never paid attention to Cornelia, whereas he told Daisy that he would marry her when she grew up. A promise was a promise, and she wouldn't be the one to break it. He would have to clearly tell her he wanted someone else before she could possibly give up.

She had risked her reputation for him, and now she was being punished by not being allowed to have her season this year. Cleverly, she had turned that edict on its head. She was now having a season in London, but with the best-looking bachelor in any season and his delightful mother who appreciated her sense of silliness. Far from being disadvantaged, she was now on top for the first time in her life.

Now that Ashford had begun to relax, she could somehow twist the situation to make him appear besotted by her. That would soon make Jake open his eyes to the woman he could have by simply lifting one finger.

During the next week, she helped Mrs. Toddington prepare to present her at the supper dance as the new, improved Daisy Gerard.

Chapter Eight

Daisy's two new evening gowns finally arrived at Ashford House. She'd ordered them to be delivered the day before the supper dance in case she needed to do any last minute alterations. All day yesterday, she'd been on tenterhooks, but as promised the gowns arrived early this morning. As she lifted each out of the box, she breathed a sigh of relief. She wanted to dash to Mrs. Toddington's room to show her, but if she planned on being a new Daisy, she should be considerably more composed. Therefore, she waited another long hour until she knew Mrs. Toddington had come down for breakfast.

"You will be proud of yourself tonight," she said as she seated herself. According to the butler, Ashford had already eaten and left the house. "My gowns are positively tasteful."

"They've arrived? I was beginning to wonder if we would need to summon the constabulary to arrest the dressmaker for making false promises." Mrs. Toddington's eyes twinkled with humour. "Are you planning to give me a preview?"

"I'm planning to surprise you tonight. You can wait, can't you?"

Her hostess nodded. "I love surprises."

Daisy did too. During the week she had received an unexpected gift from Papa of twenty pounds. The sum had covered some of the expenses for her delayed debut. He and mama had agreed that Daisy should 'come out' without going through the whole rigmarole of being presented at court. They had also agreed that she was well past the age of being shown off as a new face, since her old face had been seen by pretty well everyone she would meet as a debutante, anyway. The money that had been put aside for her would be released by her father in dribs and drabs during the next few months, as needed. He had given permission for her to stay with the Ashford family for the whole season, since Corinne still needed their full support.

For the first time, Daisy began to sympathise with her sister. Corrine had struggled with being a newly-wed and a widow within a year. She was only twenty-three years old, the age Daisy would be in two years. Daisy couldn't even imagine a married life, let alone being left a widow almost immediately. If Jake died a year into marriage, she would die herself.

Concentrating on the reality of Corrine's life, Daisy realised that being jealous of her sister for so long had become no more than a habit with which she could finally dispense. Mrs. Toddington's open-hearted acceptance of her houseguest had clearly influenced Daisy to be a better person. Her hostess accepted every kind or unkind thought Daisy expressed with an amount of consideration, which had caused her think more carefully before she judged the motives of other people. She realised that she may well not occupy the minds of others as often as she had supposed.

She'd had the smallest of conversations with Corinne, who was determined not to take the first offer she received, this time around. *"I'm holding out for the man I want," she had said, her voice expressionless.*

Since Daisy knew Corinne wanted Jake Everley, she also knew that her sister would wait forever. Normally Daisy didn't spend a second on considering Corinne's wants. Somehow, during the past month, she had changed into a better version of herself, highly influenced by Mrs. Toddington's non-judgemental ways.

"I hope the kitchen can cope. Yesterday, the cook made the pastries." Mrs. Toddington poured herself a cup of tea.

"I think the kitchen staff have everything in hand. Ashford is in control of the cellars and he said he found some treasures stored down there. We'll certainly want French champagne since this is your coming out party. Apparently the last earl didn't stint when it came to his wine collection." Mrs. Toddington added milk to her tea.

Daisy's allowance had covered almost everything, but the extra twenty pounds Papa had given her last week had certainly come in handy for new shoes, a delightful shawl made of sheer white fabric, embroidered with gold thread and tiny pearls, and the reticule she had walked past three times before deciding no female could have too many reticules.

The door opened and Ashford strode into the room wearing his riding boots and a thoughtful expression on his face. He seemed to grow more manly by the day. His breeches fitted him like a second skin, showing the hard muscles in his thighs. Gentlemen's thighs were often under discussion by young ladies, and she hadn't been responsive, not being particularly interested. Lately thighs, particularly Ashford's, came to her attention. Not only that, she'd glanced at his rear more than once, and come to the conclusion that the man had been blessed by the gods, for his body as well as his face. The only thing he lacked was human kindness. "Do you ride, Daisy?"

"I do at home, but I can't in the city, because my parents hadn't prepared for me being here, and I don't have my horse."

"I can stable your horse if you want to give me permission to have it sent to town."

She stared at him for a long moment, and finally said the words that she thought he would never earn. "That's very kind of you, sir. I will write a note this very minute giving you permission. But how will it be accomplished?"

He stood, elegantly hip-shot, tapping his crop rhythmically on the leather upper of his boot. "I will send a groom with your note and he will bring the horse back with him. Or do you think I should arrange to have a carriage transport your horse?"

"Please do. Then my horse won't get dirty on the road." She batted her eyelashes at him.

He focussed on the high ceiling and then aimed a deadly stare back at her. "One to you, if you are taking a score."

"I gave you two for the waltzing lesson. Don't complain if I catch up to you soon."

He turned and left the room.

Trying to ignore his blatant arrogance, she turned back to his mother. "Where were we?"

"Discussing food. I gather my son isn't particularly worried about his wine supply. I rather think we have little to do today other than make ourselves presentable."

"We should be driving around the park and talking to everyone we know. Apparently, that is what your son has been doing, and now he has the bright idea of encouraging me to do the same. He's rather more of a thinker than I supposed him to be," she said, trying to be fair.

"Like everyone else, he is judged by his looks. Because he is handsome, he is not expected to be anything but an adornment, and because of his stutter, he has virtually stopped speaking. His thinking apparatus has always been in good working order."

"Stutter?" Daisy completely froze.

"He has almost conquered the problem, but I suspect he works hard not to do so. We don't discuss the stutter, but I know it worries him."

Daisy swallowed the lump that had formed in her throat. She didn't think the delicious example of manhood would have a single problem. Perhaps that was the reason he didn't engage her in long conversations. Perhaps that was why he was so tolerant of Eve's stutter. He never mentioned the child's problem and he waited patiently for her to finish whatever she wanted to say. "Apparently I have misjudged him in more than one area." She gazed at the pattern of threads on her skirt.

"He speaks to the people he trusts not to belittle him. I've heard him in long conversations with his friends, but he avoids women who don't know him well. He had enough ragging during his school days to last him the rest of his life."

Daisy wanted to kick herself to death. Ashford had been kind to her. His expert guidance for the waltz had been much appreciated. He certainly deserved her understanding. She would start trying to be nice to him.

She began by smiling at him when she met him in the hallway. He stopped and stared at her with a querying expression on his face. "Why do I suddenly feel nervous?"

"You have a naturally suspicious nature."

"Only since I met you." He stared right into her eyes, and finally offered her a tentative smile, slight tilt of his lips, that grew a little wider before reducing to a pleasant quirk of his mouth.

"See. It's not so difficult to return a smile." She marched off, too impressed by his masculine beauty, slightly short of breath, but satisfied that he accepted at last her words as she meant them.

Ashford stared over the heads of his guests. The ballroom looked as glossy as any other; well, any *other* slightly-worn, smallish ballroom. The newly repaired chandeliers twinkled, spreading light in a wavering pattern on his guests, whose voices drowned out the music from the piano and two violins.

In one corner, the Gerards held court. Lady Gerard, Daisy's mother, was a sociable being, known and loved throughout the ton. Her satellite husband sorted out the riff from the raff for her. Cornelia, Daisy's sister who, pre-marriage, had dressed with frills and furbelows on everything, looked very pretty tonight in her simple, dark blue gown. Blissful, would be the word to describe the expression on her face, while she chatted to Jeremy Hastings, the earl of Delmore's younger brother, and one of Ashford's lifelong friends.

Hastings had known her forever, but this was the first time he had shown an interest in her. He had formerly dismissed her with a shrug. Ashford couldn't decide whether to laugh or frown at his friend's changed attitude. Perhaps widows interested him more than aspirants to his hand, perhaps because he could have an affair with a widow, but the rules of fair play said he shouldn't touch a young virgin.

Therefore, more often than likely, he stayed away from the younger set, unless explicitly ordered to be nice to some young lady by his sister-in-law, Anna, Lady Delmore. Hastings, despite his fair hair and angelic face, usually played by the rules and Anna was a lifelong friend of his. As Ashford was contemplating lifelong friends and young virgins, Daisy confronted him.

"Are you the master of ceremonies?"

He stared at her. "We don't need one at a private supper dance."

"I can't see a good reason for you to be hovering around the floor when you should be dancing."

"Am I expected to answer to you?" He glanced down his nose at her.

"You're expected to ask me to dance. I'm your house guest and it would only be polite."

"Have I shown you any previous examples of my courtesy?"

"Of course you have. I'm your house guest and you haven't asked me to leave."

"I've been tempted."

She ignored his words. "And you taught me to waltz. My lesson shouldn't be wasted."

"My apologies, but waltzing isn't on the program for tonight." He gazed steadily down at her. Tonight she looked like the epitome of a fashionable young lady. Her normally wispy hair had been allowed to curl on her neck and around her face, but the rest had been gathered in an unruly bunch at the crown of her head. Instead of a highly disciplined hairdo, she wore a mess that utterly suited the delicate bones of her face. As for her gown, not a touch of blue could be seen. She wore an orange gown with lace on the sleeves, so simple, yet so right for her. Tonight she outshone every other woman in the room. With the thought came a large intake of air.

"I decided to modify your list. Your mother would love to waltz. Since you love your mother, you wouldn't consider depriving her of her favourite dance."

Since his mother had ignored social functions for the better part of ten years, her son knew he was being manipulated by an expert. "Then, I must partner her," he said in voice of noble suffering.

"I doubt any of her dreams have featured waltzing with her son." Her eyebrows drew together in an expression he loved to watch, that of her frustration with him.

"But yours have?" He stared straight into her enormous eyes, and realised this might not be the right time to issue a challenge, not when he was growing more than slightly interested with her.

But instead of another trail of scattered, unanswered words, she gazed at her feet and her cheeks slowly turned pink. "For show, only. I want to look as if I have captured your interest. But not too much interest. Only enough to make a certain male wonder what he might be missing."

"I'm to be used as your bait?" He inclined his head to the side, wondering who the *certain* male might be.

Her eyes met his. "Although I don't need to compliment you, you are rather gorgeous looking. Every woman is gazing at you. Everyone will wonder why you asked me to waltz ahead of those who should be asked first."

"You certainly know how to deflate a man's ego."

"Oh, if only I could deflate yours, but that task is impossible for me. I don't have enough insults to spare."

"Well, if you promise not to fall in love with me, I can waste a few minutes of my life to dance with you."

She glanced at him and lowered her voice. "I'm half in love with you, already," she said in a fake, dreamy voice that caused a wave of longing to pass right through him.

He breathed out, knowing the brat needed a lesson or two about men, and women who tried to fool them. Leaning down from the waist to stare into her eyes, he realised he could outbluff her any day of the week. "You use the truth sparingly."

"But since I know I don't have a chance with you, you don't need to worry about me." Her eyes widened, and she took a step back.

"What makes you think you don't have a chance?" He

used a deepened tone to appear sincere and apparently did, for she blinked with surprise.

"I annoy you."

"Only when I let you."

She tried to outstare him, but her expression slowly relaxed. "I'm not sure now if you have consented to dance the waltz with me or not."

"*Not,* unless I ask you."

She whirled around and marched off. He saw her approaching Jake Everley, who had just arrived. Everley held out two hands to her, his smile wide. Ashford noted Daisy's tremulous returned smile. Her confident manner slipped as she took his offered hands. Everley indulged her with a laugh. She stared back as if she had been handed the crown jewels. Ashford realised at the moment that the brat was entranced.

Everely continued staring at her face. As luck would have it, the violins began a scratchy waltz melody. Everley searched the room with his gaze before tucking her hand under his elbow. Although he appeared to be escorting her onto the dance floor, he gracefully skirted the empty area and moved her over to her mother. After a few words, he turned to Daisy, bowed, and took *her sister's hand*, leading her onto the floor. Hastings, who had been conversing with her, was left staring at the couple, while Daisy stood, her expression desolate.

Ashford strode over to her. "I hope you don't mind, Lady Gerard, but your daughter has promised this waltz to me." He didn't wait for any answer from either lady. Instead, he bowed to Daisy. She drew a breath that lifted her shoulders, straightened her spine, and took the hand he offered to her.

He stepped into her, whirled her, and she followed him without a demur. "Don't let your feeling show," he said in a low voice. "Remember that you are half in love with me."

For a moment her face lost all expression. She blinked rapidly. Within a breath, she regained her composure. Her steps matched his and he waltzed her around the perimeter of the room, showing off her skill to all and sundry. Despite her stony face, she managed the steps with grace and charm. He wouldn't have guessed that this was the same woman who, three days ago, had stumbled over his feet and told him to stop because she was dizzy. She remembered every single dip, every single back and forward step. She followed him easily. Tonight, he was proud to be her partner.

"Are we expecting any other waltzes tonight?" he asked her in a way that shouldn't imply that he expected her to bite back.

"Just this one. I thought ..."

"That Everley would have arrived earlier?"

Her gaze met his. "You know, don't you?"

"I didn't, but I do now. He's no more in love with your sister than he is with you."

"I know that, but he chose her first." Her voice sounded bleak. "He's never done that to me before."

"He's befuddled. He has never seen you as a young lady. The realisation hit him hard. He's trying to work out what happened."

She raised a hopeful face to him. "Are you being kind, sir?"

"Have I ever been kind to you?"

"I'm not sure. When I think you are, you tell me that you had another motive, and I'm not sure what to believe."

Nor was he, but since the day he had glided over his dusty ballroom floor with her in his arms, he had the lowering thought that he liked her in a way that wasn't at all platonic. When he saw how she looked at Everley, he had experienced a moment of previously unknown jealousy. He didn't know how to accomplish the deed, but he had decided that one day the rebellious Daisy would look at him in same way. In the meantime, he had a plan that could possibly benefit him as well as her.

"You have been the bane of my life, Daisy, but since you are so determined to ruin yourself, please allow me to help."

She said through lips that barely moved, "I don't need help. I am already ruined. Why on earth do you think I'm staying with you?"

"I had wondered why you had been banished from London for the season, but I think I have f-finally spotted the reason." Normally, after the first sign of his returning stutter, he would stop and gather his thoughts, but he didn't have time. If he didn't finish the words he wanted to say, she would race off and hide in a corner somewhere. "Go along with me, and you'll soon s-see what I can do to help you."

She stared into his eyes for a long moment, and finally nodded, though her eyes turned into glints of suspicion.

"Take my arm."

She used a hesitant grip under his elbow. He turned his head and nodded at her, and began to escort her back to her mother and sister.

"Don't take me back to my family," she said in a voice

of panic. "Jake's still there, and I don't know what to say to him."

He smiled firmly and patted her hand in an avuncular way. "You will thank me, I will smile like besotted fool, and your family will draw all sorts of conclusions, none of which we shall confirm. The name of the game is mystery."

"Will you stay with me?" Her fingers clutched his arm.

"Do you want me to?"

"I don't know."

"Then, let's see what happens." He escorted her to her family group with a nonchalant expression on his face.

Her mother, who had been seated with her returned sister, smiled up at her. Everley remained by her sister's chair, his normally charming smile wary when he glanced at Daisy. "I think your next dance must be mine, Daisy," he said in a stiff voice.

"I'm sure Daisy won't mind since you are one of my best friends," Ashford said, forming an indulgent smile to aim at Daisy. "She is my house guest, you know, and my mother and I have formed quite an affection for her." He noted her panicked expression, and hesitated for a moment, trying to see if she wanted him to leave or stay.

"She is one of my best friends, too, Ashford. I think that takes priority over her being your house guest."

"I'll leave the field clear for you, but mind you save the last dance for me, Daisy."

She widened her eyes, stared at him, stared at Everley, and when the musicians struck up again for a country dance, she took his arm. Ashford grinned. The country dance would occupy the two for a quite a while, leaving him to play the host however he chose.

She saved the last dance for him and performed her part but with a look of suspicion the whole time.

For her first supper party in London for the season, Daisy had done particularly well, after the first shock of being bypassed by Jake.

Corinne hadn't been at all triumphant once she noticed Ashford's attentiveness toward her sister. "He's so beautiful," she had whispered when Ashford came to claim Daisy for the last dance. "I could look at him all day. He never misses a step in any dance. He's as graceful as any trained dancer but look at those shoulders. I don't know how you lasted in his household without being in a full swoon from the moment you wake up."

A few days ago, Daisy would have scoffed and said he was as thick as two planks, but the way he had saved her from being humiliated had changed her mind about him. Maybe he had done so for nefarious reasons, or maybe he had done so because he wasn't as insensitive as he seemed. His behaviour puzzled her.

Mrs. Toddington came down to breakfast moments after Daisy had seated herself. "I'm surprised you are out of bed so early. I assumed you would be exhausted after all that dancing."

"My feet are a little sore, but I feel quite triumphant to have had every dance taken. I noticed you didn't spend a lot of time seated, either."

"I'm rather surprised by being asked to dance. I thought

women my age would sit on the sidelines. They did when I was younger."

"Your son was also in great demand."

"He always is. He is so obliging. He would never let any woman sit out if he could help it."

Daisy glanced away, quite sure of that. The Amazing Ashford honestly puzzled her. He didn't seem to take anything for himself. He only gave. "I'm beginning to believe he is as perfect as he thinks he is."

Mrs. Toddington used one hand on her chest to help her heart to beat. "You're scaring me. Next thing, you will tell me you quite like him."

"Oh, I don't think she'll go that far, but I'm quite satisfied with being perfect." The perfect lord being discussed, pulled out his own chair and sat, leaving the footman to return to his place by the door.

"I was going to end my sentence with 'but he's not.'" Her effort to keep her composure put a strain on her neck muscles as she looked up at the beautiful earl. She willed away the flush on her cheeks, trying to keep in mind that he wasn't interested in her. He merely wanted to maintain his perfect reputation.

"I asked your mother last night about the puppet show you mentioned. The only one she recalled was performed in the garden of the former Duke of Huntsdale's town house. What made the event memorable for her was the hair pulling incident." He gazed down his nose at her as if he wanted see every spot or freckle on her face. "Apparently you have a long history of assaulting males."

She raised a patient gaze to the ceiling and back at him. "She certainly wouldn't have put me at fault."

"She merely mentioned the incident concerning you and Jake. She put the whole blame on him."

"I'm feeling rather left out here. Tell me more," his mother said pleadingly.

"Ashford will tell some sort of twisted tale to make me look bad. I will tell my version. I was sitting on the grass with my sisters watching the show when someone behind pulled my hair. And that's all."

"Your mother recalls you turning around and punching him. She said that was the start of a beautiful friendship. That's how Jake makes all his friends. He lets them punch him."

"I'll bet you never have."

"I've been tempted, but he has never pulled my hair."

"Trust me. That was his first and last time."

"There's no doubt that you are a man tamer, but I'm not sure that is the key to a man's heart. If you want my opinion ..." he hesitated.

"That was a wise move, Ashford," his mother said approvingly. "I don't think many men would have had the nerve to finish that sentence."

Daisy glanced from one to the other. "I have the feeling that I'm not a member of this club."

Mrs. Toddington smiled. "The members vary from day to day, but I like to stay on the winning team. Team Daisy for me this time around."

Ashford nodded. "Two against one. I like the odds. Therefore I will give my opinion." He waited two beats. "I think we should call on the Huntsdales today and see if the current duchess has any ideas about where to find a puppet show," he said, the coward.

"I'm so ashamed to be your mother. I thought you had more backbone."

"A wise man knows when to retreat." He smiled at Daisy, a pleasant smile, a beautiful smile; a smile that she wanted to remember for the rest of her life. He was so unnecessarily gorgeous. She acknowledged him with a nod, knowing she was the most fickle of all women. Although she would never love anyone other than Jake, she had begun to see that he wasn't the only truly kind man in the world.

She only had one problem. She'd been banned from the Huntsdale's property.

Chapter Nine

Ashford continued to calmly eat his breakfast, wanting Daisy to think he supported her in her quest for Everly's love. However, if Everley didn't make clear his intention to marry her, Ashford fully intended to sabotage any idea of romance between the two. He was sure irresponsible Everley had no such plan. He wanted Daisy to adore him without having to go the extra mile. His own pleasures always came foremost. At this stage of his life, all Everley wanted was a willing female body in his bed.

Until Ashford had been lumped with his little girls, he had been only too happy to share the beds of various experienced women while knowing he loved only Anna, his perfect woman. During the past few weeks, he had put Anna to the back of his mind. In the forefront, now lurked an annoying, rebellious miss who never stinted on the time she spent with two small children and a lonely widow. Plus, she had attributes pertaining to the female shape that he shouldn't be noticing while she was in his care. Her attributes now preoccupied his thoughts more often than not.

He frowned at Daisy, who utterly refused to join him when he called on the Huntsdales. "Don't you think it is rather arrogant of you not to visit a duchess who has certainly paid you the compliment of attending our supper dance?"

"The compliment was meant for your mother and you. I'm an incidental."

"We are a unit." He blew out a patient breath. "Every one of us organised the supper dance and we each wanted to hold it for our various reasons. What benefits one, benefits all. If my mother and I visit the Huntsdales without you, how will it appear to them?"

Daisy glanced down at her hands and began to twist a small gold bracelet around her wrist. "Tactful."

"Rude."

She raised her gaze. Her jaw tightened. "The duchess said she doesn't want to see me again until I have grown up."

His mother reached across the table and took Daisy's hand in hers. "She saw you last night, Daisy, with her eyes fully open. Perhaps she thinks you have grown up. When did you last speak to her before that?"

"The day before I was sent to you."

"Is the one event connected to the other?"

Daisy glanced down at her lap. "Yes," she said in a strangled voice to his mother. "But I don't want to tell you why."

"Is it in any way connected to Everley?" Ashford stretched out an arm and managed to lift her chin with his forefinger, encouraging her to look up into his eyes.

She twisted her head away. "You don't want to know."

He shrugged, trying to imagine a scenario involving Everley and her that would not make his fists ache to knock his friend into Kingdom Come. "I will assume that the duchess won't cut you if you arrive with us. She saw you last night and managed not to have a tantrum. Even if she hadn't forgiven you for whatever you did, she won't cut you. I doubt she spoke literally."

"Are you utterly determined to make my life miserable?"

He nodded. "I have so little else in my idle life, other than making females miserable."

"You must be very glad I'm not a man."

He nodded. "Very glad."

She tightened her jaw, scraped back her chair, and marched out of the room.

"Who won that round?" His mother looked concerned.

"I'm sure I did."

"Do you think she may be in love with Jake Everley?" She blinked and stared right through him.

"Time will tell, though I have the idea that Everley could be hard to push to the altar."

"You don't sound surprised." She scrutinised his face.

"I was initially, but I noticed how he reacted when he saw her last night, and there is definitely something brewing between the two."

"You could be right," his mother said in her thinking voice. She left the room without further ado.

Not more than sixty minutes later, the Ashford group, including the recalcitrant Daisy sat in the drawing room of the Huntsdales' town house. The tall blonde duchess was her usual composed self, and smiled warily at Daisy. "I think you chose wisely when you decided not to have a formal presentation. I so disliked my debut. So much anxiety for so little profit. I would have been much happier to have skipped the whole thing."

Her husband, the duke, frowned. "Then you wouldn't be married to me."

"If fate had meant us to be together, I would have married you anyway." The duchess made a nonchalant movement of her head.

"I don't think fate had too much to do with our marriage." Huntsdale had always been an autocrat, having inherited his title before he turned twenty-one. The only person he didn't seem to be able to control was his wife, who went her own way most of the time. Ashford enjoyed the battle of wills between the two as much as the rest of society.

She eyed her husband sideways. "Best to avoid dangerous waters, my dear."

Ashford knew the couple had married long before her season ended, but they were clearly in love. He suspected that the duke had snapped her up before anyone else could. He didn't blame the man. The duchess had become his greatest social asset during her first year as his wife. Daisy, being a Gerard, and with the Gerard ability to organise, would also be an asset to Everley. Ashford couldn't imagine the duchess not wanting her brother-in-law married and out from under her feet.

With all the aces already in play, Ashford had no idea how to keep Daisy from the man she wanted. Since he knew too much about Everley, he was determined to keep on plotting to keep them apart. In the meantime, he watched Daisy staring at the doorway as if waiting for the late-sleeping Everley to magically appear. Instead, her petite mother and sister arrived. The siblings greeted each other with a kiss and hug. Despite what Daisy said about her competitive sister, she still seemed love her. The two sat on a couch together chatting amiably while Lady Gerard headed over to him.

"I can't tell you how much I appreciate you and your mother helping Daisy to mix in society. She's very dear to me but she lives her life at a dead run, and we needed to slow her down somehow."

"I can assure you that I have been a lead-weight for her to pull."

"I didn't think she would let you down as regards to your little wards. She has always been so good with children. She has such an active mind, you see, and being surrounded by a pack of debutants would stifle her. She needs her own place in the sun, and what with her sister's problems, she would have remained in the country forever without you and your mother's delightful invitation to have her stay."

He didn't turn a hair at the inference to Daisy being invited to spend summer with him. She had been dropped on them with barely a 'goodbye.' "I can tell you that she has lightened the life of my mother considerably," he said, using the truth, unfortunately. "As for the girls, they adore her."

Mrs. Gerard's expression lightened. "I'm so pleased to see that someone other than her family can see what a treasure she is. I would hate her to be squandered on someone … oh, dear, I have lost track of what I meant to say."

Ashford now understood from whom Daisy had inherited her deviousness. From her mother. She had made sure her daughter was kept out of Everley's range by leaving her with Ashford instead. His reputation for ignoring debutants in favour of more mature women must be even more prevalent than he imagined. "If she finds a suitor while in our care, he will naturally be referred to you."

She rested a deceptively fragile hand on his forearm. "Thank you, my dear. I see have monopolised you too long. I'll leave you to the women who don't dare swarm around you while I am taking up your time."

He gazed around the room, not noting a single woman who appeared to be about to swarm around him. Lady Gerard left to join her teacup-holding cronies on the other side of the room. Ashford watched her for a moment, and then Jake Everley entered the room. He spotted Ashford, raised a hand, and marched right over, his even-featured face plastered with a smile. "Couldn't stay away, hey?"

"I was dragged here by the women folk. I'm surprised to see you out of bed so early."

"It's past midday, old chap. Actually, I didn't have a very late night. I came straight home after your supper dance."

"In time to catch your valet cavorting with the maids."

Everley laughed. "I must admit he was surprised to see me so early." His gaze wandered around the room. "Very respectable gathering here, today. Now, there's sight you don't often see—Corinne and Daisy Gerard sitting together. I think Corinne must have changed since her widowhood. In the normal run of things, she wouldn't speak to Daisy when she has other people around. She has always been very competitive, whereas Daisy seems puzzled that her sister sees her as a threat."

Ashford stared at the sisters. Now he knew Daisy, he wouldn't give Corrine a second glance, but he had previously thought Corinne was rather pretty, and couldn't understand Daisy's perpetual mocking of the relationship between the two. "So, that's why she is such a pest."

Everley took a step back to aim a repressive glare at him. "She is not a pest. I will meet you tomorrow at dawn unless you take that back."

Ashford gave a scoffing laugh. "You have only seen dawn when you have been tossed out of some dive early in the morning."

Everley drew his eyebrows together, apparently trying for a considering expression. "I wonder why we don't have pistols at midday?"

"The constabulary doesn't approve of people killing each other in daylight."

"Oh, well, in that case, I suppose I will have to withdraw my challenge." Everley scratched his ear. "Do you honestly not like her?"

Ashford shrugged. "She tends to grow on one—like some sort of obnoxious parasite."

Everley punched his upper arm. "Be polite to her, or you will deal with me."

Ashford moved with his reprobate friend toward the Gerard sisters. "I plan to take a lesson from you on how to be charming."

"You bastard," Everley said in an undertone. "Even without bothering to be charming, you still manage to keep women crowding around you."

"Silence is a man's best friend."

No one knew more about the power of silence than a stutterer, which Everley should, having been his friend for so many years. During that time, Everley had spoken for Ashford when words had been sought but not found. This meant Everley would be his friend forevermore. Ashford hoped he was right in that his friend didn't mean to marry Daisy. If he truly loved the woman Ashford now wanted, he would bow out. But first he would need irrefutable proof of that love.

With his friend he stood in front of the sisters, who uniformly raised two gazes. Daisy smiled at Everley, her eyes shining with adoration. Everley would take that as his due. Ashford would fall into a dead faint if she glanced at him like that.

But the race was not over until the final lap. "Everley noticed that neither of you has a cup of tea." He glanced at Everley.

His friend sighed, turned, and signalled to a waiting maid who came over. "Tea for two," he said, "Unless Lord Ashford wants a cup, as well."

Ashford nodded and smiled at Corinne. "Should I call you Lady Standing?" he asked as he sat on the couch beside her.

She dimpled. "Should I call you Lord Ashford?"

"Since you put it that way, I shall continue to call you Corinne." He gave her his innocent smile, the one he kept for merry widows, though he doubted she would ever fit that description, being closer to meek than outrageous like her sister. "I'm used to being called Toddie, and I am happy for you to continue doing so."

"You call me Daisy, but you have never said I could call you Toddie," Daisy said in an outraged voice.

He adored that tone from her. Every single time she overreacted, his heart filled with joy. "You can continue to call me Ashford, since you have never known me as Toddie."

Her jaw dropped. He hoped she would continue to argue, but she remembered she was out to impress Everley. She dropped her gaze, and the 'pah' she probably meant to say, turned into, "P," which in itself was quite enough to express her thoughts. He wanted to wrap his arms around her and stay that way for a moment or two while he enjoyed the ceasing of her huffing and puffing.

"You can continue to call me Jake for the rest of your life," Everley said, sounding put out. "After all, we have been friends for the whole of your life."

She looked up at him. "Ashford should give up his place on the sofa so that you can sit beside me."

"He will want to sit next to Corinne." Ashford used his puzzled expression. "I can't see a place beside you."

"You don't need to give up your seat to Jake. He lives here," Corinne said to him, glancing at her sister. "He can bring over a chair if he wishes to speak to both of us."

Everley took this sisterly banter as a normal part of his day, which added to Ashford's amusement. He would remain glued to this seat for as long as this competition between the sisters lasted, although he suspected that Daisy would be the winner, for she had the most to win. He doubted that Corinne was interested in Everley. When Jeremy Hastings arrived on the scene, she immediately vacated her seat to be introduced to Lady Delmore,

Ashford's only love. He smiled at Anna while inwardly holding his breath. These incidental meetings hurt less each time. Eventually he would be able to put her in the back of his mind. In the meantime, he had Daisy's ructions to enjoy. He turned back to her.

She stared from him to Anna, her expression suspicious, but she didn't speak. Finally she took a deep breath and began another ridiculous conversation with Everley, concerning the time when she saw the puppet show in his garden. "Not here," Everley said, crossing his arm over his chest. "I've never seen a puppet show at Huntsdale House."

"Mama said it was here. Have you ever known my mother to be wrong? You pulled my hair so you must have been sitting behind me."

"I have never pulled your hair."

"A hundred times," she said, smugly. "At least."

"Why do I feel I am back in my nursery?" Ashford rubbed his forehead. "I think I will join the adults." He stood. The arguers stared at him in unison.

Everley stood up, too. "I'll come with you."

"Then I will have no reason to leave."

"I'll go with Jake." Daisy stood as well.

Ashford clapped his palm on his forehead and groaned. "Stay, both of you, until you can stop your squabbling. I'll ask around and find a puppet show if I have to die in the attempt." He brushed his hands together, indicating he was done with them, but of course, he had an ulterior motive for leaving them together.

Those two couldn't work out a lover's assignation if he left them alone for a hundred years. Their heads were filled with 'what was' rather than 'what could be.' If Daisy planned to make Jake propose to her, she would need to learn adult tactics. Closing his eyes for a moment, he realised he would be only too pleased to teach her a trick or two.

Somehow Mrs. Toddington managed to obtain an invitation that night to a small gathering of young people. Daisy mentioned this to Smithson, while her hair was being twisted into shape for this evening's entertainment at the house of Lady Charrington.

"It's my lord who would have been invited."

"No, Mrs. Toddington received the invitation."

Smithson gazed down the length of her nose at Daisy. "Because people want Lord Ashford at their functions."

"What makes you think that?"

"Aside from below stairs conversations, I have eyes, don't I? I don't think there is a more handsome single gentleman in the upper echelons."

"Handsome?" Daisy laughed scathingly. "Handsome is as handsome does."

Smithson frowned. "God would certainly want him to join his choir of angels," she said staunchly.

"Not if He knew how Ashford behaved." Daisy crossed her arms. She didn't like to think that the servants discussed his looks, despite the fact that she'd always garnered her juiciest gossip from the servants. "Do they know that he flirts with everyone?" Did they know that he had waltzed with her and made her heart clench in her chest? Did they know that this morning she'd had a hard time concentrating on Jake once Ashford had left the conversation?

"He always behaves like a perfect gentleman. He doesn't pinch the maids, he doesn't raise his voice, and he is the perfect son and guardian to those dear little girls."

"Ah, but when he is out, he is surrounded by females. He doesn't bother with one. He wants them all. I call that greedy."

"Oh. Well, no one is perfect. If he can have all the women, I don't see why he shouldn't."

Daisy disapproved of Smithson's attitude. Ashbury certainly shouldn't take so much advantage of his looks. He should rely on his character, first. A man needed to be decent, generous, kind, and thoughtful. He certainly wasn't the first mentioned. A decent man wouldn't have the effect on her that he had. She wouldn't have begun to notice his body if he were decent. His manners would be more important but she couldn't notice the non-existent.

Then at the gathering, she noticed Ashford's effect on women. Being from a household with a majority of women, she recognised the mute passing of messages from one woman to another, a widening of eyes when he passed, the even more subtle hidden smile, women being more conscious of their posture, and few pinker than normal cheeks. She had the urge to snatch his arm and march him right out again, until she realised his handsomeness wasn't his fault. He was only as beautiful as his mother and as attractive as his father must have been. The combination had turned out to be incredible.

Although she and Mrs. Toddington had been invited to a small gathering, the word 'small' seemed rather inappropriate when at least a hundred people had come together to socialise either on the dance floor or in a side room to play cards. She didn't mind a good game of cards herself, but she would rather use her pin money otherwise. "I can't say I know too many people here tonight. The young people look more like newlyweds than debutantes."

"Are you worried about the lack of prospective suitors?" Ashbury asked, his tone speculative.

She groaned. "Naturally. I can hardly sleep at night wondering when my prince charming might arrive."

"He could be standing right in front of you." He stood in front of her.

"Is this your gauche way of asking me to dance with you?"

"Ash. Stop teasing her." His mother pushed her finger into his hard chest. "Either ask her to dance or go away."

"I never thought I would hear such harsh words from my own mother." He let his eyelids drop leaving his shocking eyelashes to rest on his cheeks. At the same time he held out his hand for Daisy to accept. "Let me show you off on the dance floor now and I will be able to leave for the card room. I don't doubt you will have many other chaps asking to you dance after they have seen you on the floor."

"Is that a compliment I just heard?"

He grabbed her hand, swung her around and before she knew what had happened, she was in a cotillion with him. She lost sight of his mother. By the time she had almost exhausted her vocabulary speaking politely to each gentleman whose hand she took during the dance, she realised that having a season was easier than she had supposed. One delightful young man asked her to reserve a country-dance with her before he swung her into her next partner.

Ashbury escorted her off the floor into a group of young gentlemen. By the time he disappeared, her next two hours had been promised for various other dances. However, she lost sight of Ashbury. During a rather long break, Mrs. Toddington left her with a group of other ladies Daisy's age or older. For reasons only known to the god of improvidence, her sister Corinne joined her group. Daisy sighed. Clearly, Mama had also arrived. She smiled politely, which caused her sister's eyebrows to reach her hairline. "Not expecting me, were you?" Corinne said with a nauseatingly sweet smile.

"No, but I am utterly delighted to see you at *every* single event I attend."

The other ladies greeted Corinne with a welcome that set Daisy apart from the crowd. Not being married, widowed, and even an old debutante, she knew none of the gossip that Corinne did. However, the ladies left her in no doubt that Ashbury made the hearts of even older married women pulse with excitement.

"As for Jake Everley, did you hear that he is about to be betrothed?" asked a woman who had been introduced to her as Lady Mandleham.

"No," Daisy said in a horrified voice. "Who?" she said like an owl with a sore throat.

"That Venning girl. She's fast. He likes fast women."

"I've heard that he prefers married women," Corrine said, shrugging her shoulders.

Lady Mandleham, laughed. "No. That's Ashford. He is currently making Lady Constance a very happy wife."

Daisy's jaw dropped low enough to hit her chest. For a moment, she had to concentrate on breathing. Finally, she managed a disapproving frown. "I don't know how he can spare the time." She raised her chin.

"He hasn't been in town for months, and she was moping around, and now look at her. That feline has her cream."

Daisy stared where the lady indicated and saw Ashford standing too close to a beautiful woman with golden hair, perfect white skin, and mouth too red not to have been coloured. Her hand rested on Ashford's forearm and her gaze melted into his. She wore a gown made from delicate lace with an indecent under-gown that showed the full outline of her body. Daisy's eyes widened enough to hurt. "She is old," she said, because she couldn't see a single imperfection on the lady who was easily the most beautiful woman she had ever seen.

"Forty, I believe," said Lady Gossip. "Her husband is in his sixties. I suspect she is too much for him to handle, but Ash …" She stopped and blinked after staring at Daisy's expression. "I suspect I am merely repeating gossip. No one really knows about their relationship but because they are both so beautiful, we like to think they have paired up. That way, we don't have to underrate ourselves."

Daisy swallowed. "I'm sure he wouldn't be involved in anything dishonourable. He is also kind to his servants, people who annoy him, and children."

The lady laughed. "That's the problem. He is too perfect to be real."

"He is not exactly perfect," Daisy began, but a hand grasped hers. She turned. "Jake. Are you here?"

"That's a redundant question, Daisy. If you have nothing better to do, would you mind joining me on the dance floor?"

For the first time in her life, she didn't leap to Jake's command. "My feet are practically worn out. If it's another country dance, no."

"It is another country dance."

"Find someone else."

"Certainly," he said in a stiff voice. "If that's the way you feel, I'll leave you to your conversation. Oh, before I go, did you find out about the puppet show?"

"Not yet."

He marched off, leaving her wondering about her contrariness tonight. Normally she would leap at the opportunity to hold his hand. The very idea having him in her sights for the full length of a cotillion had been her life-long dream.

"You refused Lord Everley?" Lady Mandleham's eyes rounded as she turned back to Daisy.

"He's a family friend," Corrine said, her voice haughty. "He wouldn't mind in the least. He probably would prefer to be in the card room than to be dancing with Daisy."

A flicker of a frown crossed Lady Mandleham's face. "I hope you don't mind me asking, but what was that Everley said about a puppet show?"

"Lord Ashford has two young nieces who have never seen a puppet show." Daisy said, annoyed about Corrine's interruption. "I promised them they would see one in London."

"It so happens that I will have a group of puppeteers putting on a show in my garden tomorrow for my young son and daughter. You would be welcome bring Lord Ashford's nieces."

"Do I hear my name being mentioned?"

"In relation to a puppet show," Daisy explained, not wanting Ashford to think people had been discussing him. "I'm going to take Eve and Dawn to Mrs. Mandleham's tomorrow." She indicated the woman, who nodded.

Ashford held out his hand to her. Without a thought, she gave him hers, and found herself swung into another cotillion. As usual he performed with grace and charm. He smiled at her each time they met in the centre and took each others' hand. Each time his smile brought the same thumping of her heart. She tried to steel herself, but she had grown to like him very much. In fact, too much. The thought of him with another woman, occupying her bed, brought out the stark horror of jealousy, uncontrollable jealousy: jealousy that piled on hurt. She didn't know how she could charm him or be beautiful enough to compete with his lovers. Anyway, why would she? She was in love with Jake and would surely marry him one day.

That night she slept fitfully, and awoke, knowing she had dream after dream and none remained in her foggy head. All she knew was that her brain had fuzzed into scenes she needed to recall but couldn't. Smithson made sure she dressed carefully for breakfast and that her hair sat tidily in place.

Her visit to the nursery was chaotic that morning. After informing the girls about the upcoming treat, she'd been almost hugged to death. Smithson's work on her hair being quickly wasted, she made sure that the girls had shiny clean faces and brushed curls. They wore the new dresses, one in pink and the other in yellow, both of which had been purchased for them yesterday.

Ashford arrived in the nursery wearing a dashing jacket in dark blue with black lapels. His breeches clung to his muscular thighs, where she couldn't look for any amount of time, and his long boots had been as highly polished as his sparkling white teeth. Her face warmed with an unlikely maidenly blush because her thoughts had become less pure than ever before, this morning. He made her crave the sight of night-tousled black hair, a sleepy morning smile, and a welcoming embrace, none of which would be offered to her in her lifetime. Her chest emptied with pain of regret. "As you can see, we are all ready."

"Have your breakfast, Daisy? Mother is awaiting you."

"Have you had yours?"

"I ate before my morning ride. If we want to be at the puppet show in time to find a seat, I suggest we leave within the next half hour."

"Are you coming too, sir?" Eve asked, her face a picture of surprise.

"I wouldn't miss a puppet show for the world. Miss Daisy found this one for us and I simply have to attend."

Daisy left the nursery to the sound of delighted squeals and unanswerable questions, through which he would bluff his way. She finished her breakfast quickly, discovering that Mrs. Toddington had plans for the day and didn't mean to attend the puppet show. "The thought of sitting in the grass amid wriggling children doesn't appeal to me, Daisy. I have a gown fitting today."

Therefore, Daisy and Ashford, with two excited little girls, arrived in a manner timely enough to find a place on the scythed grass in a gracious garden amid a wriggling mass of children with their attendant maids or older siblings. A few parents also attended. And air of excitement hushed the crowd as they watched three people enter a booth decorated with red and yellow painted canvas.

Ashford sat with his legs outstretched gazing indulgently at the children.

Daisy averted her gaze, trying to watch the puppet show, but her whole being focussed on Ashford. Once she'd been totally in love with Jake, but she knew now she hadn't experienced real love. She had liked Jake because he was her knight in shining armour, taking her side when no one else would. The feelings she had for him were pure hero worship.

Ashford was another matter entirely. She could easily hero worship a man who was kind to everyone, and she could worship him for the looks with which he'd been blessed. She sighed and gazed at her shoes, knowing she didn't want to love a man that everyone else loved, but she did. She loved him for his kindness, for his sense of the ridiculous, and for his open heart. More than that, she loved him because she did.

Chapter Ten

"M-mama said you shouldn't hit p-people with sticks." Her expression righteous, Eve wriggled herself into the carriage seat.

Daisy plopped down beside her, followed closely behind by Dawn. "Your mama was right." Although she agreed with the sentiment, this was the first time either of the girls had mentioned their mother in her presence. "Mr. Punch was wrong, but he hit people to make them aware of..."

"The uselessness of violence," Ashford finished in a sanctimonious tone, which Daisy knew to be faked. He didn't have a righteous bone in his whole gorgeous body. If he had, he would have made far more of her appalling behaviour instead of constantly letting his eyes light up with secret amusement. The pale sunlight gleamed off his smooth shaven skin.

She watched him take a forward seat with his usual easy grace.

"I didn't like the hitting part, but the rest was funny." Daisy grinned at Eve. "Which part did you like the best?"

"When Mrs. Judy hit Mr. Punch."

Daisy repressed the laugh that sat inside her.

Dawn wriggled in her seat, and said, "I liked the baby. She looked like my doll, Beatrice."

"The resemblance was astounding." Ashford crossed his arms. "Except for her face and the body."

His dry comment made Daisy want to burst with laughter, but she couldn't when the current conversation might lead to clues about the whereabouts of the girls' mother. Sidetracking would lead nowhere. "Did your mama say that to Dawn as well?"

"Eve was trying to hit me with a stick. Mama said not to."

"Perhaps Eve was too little to understand."

"She was four."

"I was not. I was three."

"You always say you were three."

"I wonder why you chose that age?" Daisy said to Eve.

"Because she likes the number. She hasn't celebrated another birthday since." Dawn's mouth quivered and she stared out the window at the passing scenery.

Daisy grabbed her up and hugged her. Eve threw herself into the bundle of hugs too. Ashford exchanged glances over their heads with Daisy, who'd always had a mother and a father but never until this moment had she known how lucky she had been. Her parents loved and supported her brother and her sisters, and wouldn't have considered leaving them, no matter what. Her heart ached for these adorable children, who missed their mother so much that they couldn't even express their sorrow except by making safe nests to sleep in at night. Daisy swallowed the lump in her throat, wishing she could make promises about finding the girls' mother.

Ashford stared out the window while the barouche slowly moved through the crowded streets. Finally the girls settled back into their seats and copied him by staring over his shoulder and pointing out various inconsistencies in the people in the streets, like striped trousers, tall hats, and a woman who could barely carry the goods in her basket. Finally reaching the townhouse, both children sprang out and raced into the drawing room to tell Mrs. Toddington all about the puppet show.

Ashford held Daisy back. "That's the first time either child has mentioned her mother to me. Do they talk about her to you?"

Daisy shook her head. "I assumed she was one of your lovers."

"One? How many do you think I have?" He glared at her.

"You don't have to have them all at the same time. You can have one after the other."

"I'm glad to hear that. Is this your rule, or did you read it in the book of lovers?"

She hissed an impatient sigh between her teeth. "It's common sense. It's hard enough to love one person without filling your brain with another." For no known reason, her gaze dropped.

The patterns on the floor tiles in the entrance turned into a blur of colours. Since the age of ten, she had expected to marry Jake, because that was when he had told her he would. "Dash and damn Miss Alice Renfrey," he'd said when he had marched into her parent's country house on a beautiful summer's day. He'd come down from Oxford to stay with her parents for the holidays.

She'd reached out and held his hand. "If that mean girl is being nasty to you, refer her to me. I will put spiders in her hair."

He had laughed and hugged her. "My dear intrepid Daisy. You aren't even afraid of spiders. This makes you the only girl for me."

"You can only hug girls you want to marry," she'd said in a hopeful voice, appreciating his hug. Corinne had been taunting her about something or other.

He had stepped back and said, "I don't doubt I will want to marry you when you are older."

She'd accepted that as his proposal, but of course she couldn't tell her parents. Who would believe that ten year-old girl had accepted the hand of an eighteen year-old duke's brother? Who would believe that girl had taken his supportive words as a proposal of marriage? She now wished she hadn't, and she wished she hadn't made a spectacle of herself last month and been caught by the duchess. She had been a fool. However, if she hadn't, she wouldn't be in sitting in carriage with a lovely lord and two fractured children.

Her mind flittered here and there, trying to find a way to help the girls as regards to their mother. Ashford had also been silenced by Dawn's revelation. Daisy turned to him. "When did you employ Mary?" she asked quietly.

"I inherited her with the girls." He stared at her for a

long minute before he frowned and smacked his palm on his forehead. "I think it's time I had a real conversation with her." He glanced at the girls and back to Daisy, as if warning her not to begin an adult conversation in front of them.

"I think we should bring one of the kittens upstairs to play today."

Two sets of widened eyes turned to Daisy. "Inside?" Dawn said in a surprised voice. "Mary said we don't keep animals in the house."

"Just this once." Daisy knew who would be cleaning up any mess the kitten would make—not her. But she didn't want to be too inconsiderate toward Mary, who would pay her back in an underhanded way like not getting the girls washed and dressed in time for breakfast with the adults. She'd done that once already when Daisy had gone to the stables to see the kittens too, which had likely made her meeting with the groom less likely.

Mrs. Toddington began to suffer the retelling of the Punch and Judy show by the girls with an indulgent smile on her face. Ashford left the room. Daisy followed him. "Are you going to speak to Mary now?"

"I'll have her sent to my study."

"I want to be with you. I might ask questions you don't think of."

Ignoring her, he beckoned over a footman. "Tell the nursery maid to come to my study, please." He turned.

Before he could escape, she linked her arm with his. He stared into her eyes long enough to make her drop her hold and marched off. She followed. When he reached his study, she hastened into the room before he could block her with his arm. In triumph, she sat in one of the armchairs that faced the window. His desk was positioned in front. "You should sit at the desk. That will make you more lordly."

He bowed with a flourish like a courtier and obeyed her order with a mock insolent expression on his face. Framed by the sunshine glittering through the dust on the pane of the window, he sat in silence. Hasty footsteps preceded the arrival of Mary who hurried into the room, her forehead creased with anxiety. "Yes, my lord," she said a breathless voice as she halted in front of his desk, her fingers twisted together.

"Sit," he said, indicating the chair beside Daisy.

Mary gave Daisy a wide-eyed glance before sitting on the edge of chair, her hands clasped in her lap. Like Daisy, she faced the imposing mahogany desk, where the silent lord sat rearranging his blotter.

He raised his gaze. For the first time, Daisy saw him in a different light. Far from being a pretty toy, he had transformed himself into an imposing figure, with rigid posture and a severe expression on his face. "How long have you been in my employ?" he asked in a haughty voice.

"Nigh on three months, my lord." Mary's voice quivered.

"Why have you never come to me with worries about the children?"

Daisy's eyes widened. She would have asked about their mother.

"I'm not worried about the girls, not now. They're well fed, well dressed, and happy."

"Surely, they would be happier if they had their mother beside them?"

Mary nodded, clearly puzzled. "But she left."

"Why?"

"She didn't tell me. She said she was going to see her parents. She said she would be back in a week."

"Did you tell this to the former Lord Ashford?"

"Yes, my lord."

"How long did you wait after she left until you contacted him?"

"Two weeks, sir."

"And he had them for three months before he died? Correct?"

"Yes, my lord."

"Did he make any attempt to find her?"

"I expect so. He said her parents hadn't seen her."

Ashford heaved a breath. "Where do you think she went?"

Mary stared at her lap. "Home, as she said. She needed money. I thought she wanted to beg her parents to take her back."

"But she didn't say that to you?"

"No. But she wouldn't. Not to me. I'm a nursery maid, not her personal maid."

"Did you tell this to the former Lord Ashbury?"

"Yes."

"And what did he do?"

"I don't know. He was ill. I don't think he did anything. At least, he didn't tell me anything. And then he died and you and Mrs. Toddington arrived."

Ashbury rearranged the papers on his desk. "That's all," he said, rising to his feet. "You may go back to your duties."

Mary scuttled out of the room like a cockroach caught in the lamplight.

Daisy sighed. "That was a waste of time."

Ashbury shrugged. "At least their mother left willingly. I assume the former earl spoke to her parents, and I shall do the same."

After speaking to Mary the night before, Ashford had decided to see if he could track down Mrs. Emerson, himself. He packed and left during the mid morning. He'd had possession of the Emerson children for two months. In that time, he had done nothing about finding their mother, assuming she had run away with a lover, or even wanted to migrate without the burden of her children.

Last night, he'd read through all the relevant correspondence between the former earl and the children's maternal grandfather who, by rights, should take custody of the girls. However, according to the only letter that Mr. Ethridge, the girl's grandfather, had written, he was in no position to bring up small children. No reason had been mentioned. Ashford wanted to speak to him to find out what else he may have known about his daughter's life that could be useful in Ashford's search for her.

In his curricle, accompanied by his groom, he relaxed his horses into a slow trot. The sunlight dappled the tree-lined road ahead. He enjoyed mild weather during the morning, and arrived in Reigate in the mid afternoon. Mr. Ethridge owned a modest estate on the edge of the village. The word 'estate' was an exaggeration, though the small manor house appeared to be well kept, with clipped hedges lining the carriageway. He pulled up in the turning circle in front of a two storey building. Before he sprang down from his curricle, the sturdy front door opened, and a manservant appeared.

Ashford strode toward him. "I'm hoping to see Mr. Ethridge. I'm Ashford, the current guardian of his grandchildren."

The man bowed. "This way, sir. Mr. Ethridge is poorly today and taking the sun in the solarium. I'll let him know you are here."

Ashford waited in an attractive, but old fashioned morning room, with faded curtains and worn carpet on the floor. He examined the view through distorted glass window, delighted to see a rose garden. Mrs. Emerson had been brought up in what he saw as a pleasant household. A slight rumbling sound preceded the opening of the door. A chair on wheels containing a very old gentleman creaked into the room. "Good afternoon, Lord Ashford. I'm Ethridge."

Ashford moved over to shake the frail offered hand. "I'm here regarding the disappearance of your daughter."

A gentle voice said, "You've found her?" Two grey eyebrows lifted.

"Not yet. I've just started the search for her. I must apologise for my laxity. I made an assumption that my predecessor had explored all avenues, but apparently his investigation was halted by his bad health."

"His man told me he asked at the stop where she disappeared. No one seemed to have noticed her." The gentleman shook his head. His eyes glistened. "It's a bad business. Very bad. She wouldn't have run off. She adored her children. I would have taken them but my wife died a week after Mary disappeared." He hung his head, twisting his fingers together. "I'm afraid I am not coping well with her death yet."

"My condolences, sir." Ashford sat in silence with the new widower for a moment, wondering where to take the conversation from there. He heaved a sigh, and ploughed on. "I'm not here to discuss the disposal of the girls. I would much prefer to find their mother, if possible. You say she wouldn't have run off. Were you in constant contact with her?"

"We wrote letters to each other every month. She was grieving for her husband and couldn't manage. Her mother and I had almost decided she should come back home to live, but she wanted to talk to me about the arrangement. She set off. And that was that. No one has seen her since."

Ashford stared at his knees and thought for a while. The old gentleman, being a blood relative of the girls, would be a more suitable guardian than a new earl, but he was a good twenty years older than Ashford had expected. The man must be in his eighties. The new earl had a mother in her late forties who adored the girls. The die had been cast. He would keep the girls if he couldn't find their mother.

"I eat early," the old man said. "Would you care to join me for a high tea?"

Ashford nodded. "Thank you. Tonight, I plan to stay at the inn where Mrs. Emerson disappeared. I will make extensive inquiries there and keep in contact with you about my findings."

During the next hour, he made arrangements for Mr. Ethridge to visit Ashbury Hall when the London season ended, to make sure he approved of the living arrangements for his grandchildren. The next hour passed swiftly while he listened to helpful memories of the children's mother, who appeared to have been a careful parent.

Finally, with an old water-coloured painting of Mrs. Emerson in his possession, he took the road back to the King's Ransom, the inn where she had disappeared. Fortunately, he found a good room on the upper floor with an annex for his groom. He ate alone.

The next morning he wandered down to the taproom. A weary faced barmaid served him a substantial breakfast of ham and bread with ale to wash down the crumbs. As the maid came to take his plates, he smiled at her. She stood staring at him, which he tried not to let annoy him. He knew very well how he looked and that women admired his face, but he had long grown tired of unearned admiration. "I would like a coffee, when you have a moment to spare."

The maid glanced around the room as if searching for another customer. "Right away, sir."

"Before you go ..." He smiled again, well aware of effect of his smiles. "Some weeks ago, a woman disappeared in this vicinity. I believe she stepped out of the carriage here, to use the amenities. Do you know anything about the matter?"

"As you said, she disappeared. I don't know where she went, and so I told the other gentleman who enquired."

"So, you were working here that day?"

"Yes, my lord." She appeared wary.

"Do you remember seeing her?"

The maid nodded. "I saw her go into the outhouse, but I was busy and didn't notice her leaving."

Ashford flipped a gold coin out of his pocket. "Would

you mind taking me on tour outside. I need to see where she might go from the outhouse."

"The old gentleman's servants have already looked."

"It would do any harm for me to also look, would it?"

She bobbed a curtsey. "No, my lord. I'll take you now, before the place starts to get busy."

He stood and followed her to the front door. She took him to the coach-yard and then headed to a side path that trailed through spindly trees to an outhouse. Inside, he saw nothing but a long bench, holding a stack of bourdaloue.

"We keep this clean for the ladies. She came in here and disappeared."

Ashford glanced around the tidy area and noticed the outhouse had another door at the side. Since no one had seen her leave, the possibility existed that she had gone in one door and left by the other. "Thank you. I'm sure you are too busy to continue to show me around. But before you leave, did any other coach arrive at the same time as Mrs. Emerson's?"

The maid adopted a thinking face. "I really can't remember, sir. Coaches come and go at all times of the day. I wouldn't have remembered Mrs. Emerson if she hadn't asked me to prepare a pot of tea for her. I did, and waited for her to come back, but by that time the coachman was already searching for her. Come to think of it, I think another coach left about that time."

Ashford's next stop was outside the coaching house. He finally found a groom who remembered the incident. "We had plenty of trade that day, Milord. Coaches stopping all morning. I don't remember the order, but we had at least three coaches in the yard when she disappeared. One belonged to Mr. Fraser who was on his way home from town."

Before he left the inn, Ashford went on a hunt through the surrounding woods, but of course he found no sight of the woman. Many trampling feet had taken the same path searching for her and he was unlikely to find a clue.

Chapter Eleven

Ashford didn't want to waste his time on the road. Nothing he had asked anyone had given him a single clue that might lead to Mrs. Emerson's discovery. However, he decided to check at other post carriage stops, just in case. Finding in himself an exhilarating sense of determination, he pulled up at the next on his list, The Dicing Pig, although he knew his task to be problematical.

Beginning with his former spiel to the welcoming proprietor about a missing woman and the approximate date—he had no real date, for no one remembered that small detail—he halted when he saw a frown appear on the man's face. "Although I agree you can pick morsels of gossip at posting stops, you'd be better off tryin' elsewhere."

Ashford raised his eyebrows in query. "For example?"

"The local midwife picks up most of the gossip 'round here. If anything happened, you would be sure to 'ear it from her."

After obtaining the midwife's address, he headed back the way he had come and entered the village of Cumber. Although the directions had been imprecise, he found the midwife quickly, for the first person he stopped to ask pointed at the row of houses in which the midwife resided. He identified the exact dwelling by a mother sitting with a squalling baby on the shady porch. "Not often we see gennilmen around here," the woman said, her eyes narrowed with suspicion. She turned her head and shouted at the open doorway. "Hey, Mavis, you have a customer."

A woman with a crumpled linen mobcap appeared. "Yes, sir," she said, staring at him, wearily. "Did the doctor send you?"

He shook his head, offering her the smile that caused the ladies in London to stare at him with fluttering eyelashes. For that very reason, he rarely used this smile. The situation seemed to call for him to be charming rather than overt. "I'm looking for a relative who disappeared about three to four months ago. I was told you know everyone, and might have heard a word or two that might help me. Do you know of anyone who arrived in the village about that time?"

After she had stared at him with narrowed eyes, and blinked a few times, she heaved a deep breath. "As long as this doesn't involve breaking a confidence, I'll hear you out." Her hand indicated a small room furnished with worn chairs and a side table holding a lamp, a pile of folded rags, and a jug.

He removed his top hat and settled on a hard horsehair chair and leaned forward, trying to adopt an aura of responsibility. "A distant relative of mine, by the name of Mrs. Julia Emerson, stepped out of a mail coach to use the amenities at the Kings' Ransom to … relive herself, and has never been seen since. She has two young daughters who miss their mother. I promised I would help them if I could."

She shook her head. "I'm afraid I don't know anyone by that name."

He ferreted around in jacket pocket and found the miniature given to him by her father. "I believe this is a good likeness."

She blinked and stared at the painting for some time, moving the angle into the light from the small window. "I think I may have seen this woman in the village. I'm not sure who she is, but she works for Mr. Davies."

"Where can I find Mr. Davies?" He rose to his feet, ready to leave

"He owns a small farm down Longbottom way."

"Could you direct me, please, Mrs. Smith?" He used his eyes the way he had never tried before, filling them with what he hoped looked like blatant pleading.

She glanced away. Perhaps he had overdone his lost puppy expression, for she stared at him as if he was a nice juicy apple that she longed to try. He blinked, took back his pride, and she grinned at him.

After she had drawn a crude map on a piece of scrap paper, he climbed into his phaeton again.

Daisy had no idea she would miss Ashford so much. He'd been away for only three days and yet her every thought was of him—had he eaten, had he slept comfortably, did he miss her? The last thought preyed on her mind more than the others. During the past weeks they had been in London, he had been extremely courteous to her, more attentive than to anyone else. He made sure she had dancing partners, but he also made sure he partnered her.

Lately, when they danced together, the world had begun to stand still. She could concentrate only on him. She knew her gaze was hopelessly fixed on his. She also knew that he searched her out more than he had. When she was with him, her heartbeat fluctuated between thunderous and unsteady, and the rest of the world turned invisible. This didn't happen to her with anyone else, even Jake.

For years she'd thought of no man but Jake, who had suddenly turned into a family friend rather than a prospective husband. She should have seen him that way from the start. Although his eyes lit up when he saw her, they lit with amusement, not adoration. Ashford's smile held a special gleam, not only amusement, but also genuine appreciation.

Just as a test, she smiled at her current dancing partner the way she had begun to smile at Ashford. The man widened his eyes with shock and smiled back. Corrine would have had fits, for no one smiled at a dancing partner in any way but politely. Only 'fast' women did, but as a matter of fact, Daisy was 'fast.' She'd been in Jake's bed. Fortunately, he hadn't been home at the time, but Daisy's intentions were in no way related to purity.

If she could visit Jake's bed, she could certainly occupy Ashford's even if an invitation wasn't forthcoming. She sighed. She couldn't do that to him. If she were to be caught, he would be blamed and forced to ask for her hand.

Her concentration wavered, and she caught her heel in the flounce at the hem of her gown. Although she continued to move on to new partners in the country dance, she knew she had ripped the fabric. Before she could decide what to do, she glanced at her next partner.

For a moment she couldn't focus. She appeared to be delusional, wanting Ashford and seeing him where he couldn't possibly be—standing right before her. He gave his inimitable grin, the one that said 'hello' and 'what do you think you are doing?' in the same expression.

"You're back," she said superfluously.

"Am I?" He held out his hand to her, his eyes hooding.

She clasped her fingers around his, and found herself being led off the dance floor. After a brief glance behind her, she followed where he led. People stared and she willed her cheeks not to redden. He turned when she pulled back slightly. "What's wrong?"

"Do I look like a child about to be chastised?" she said in a careful voice.

"You look like a lady who is about to leave a room with a gentleman."

"In other words, I am about to cause a scandal."

"Are you my ward?"

"No, I'm your guest."

"Well, that's all right then. Gentleman are allowed to remove their guests from a ballroom if they have some information to pass on."

She pulled him to a halt, trying to look shocked.

"You're not going to propose to me, are you?" She only half-meant her words as a joke.

He widened his beautiful, dark eyes with surprise. "Not yet."

Her jaw loosened and her heartbeat stepped up. 'Not yet' sounded as if he would, sometime. Her throat drying, she nodded, taking her hand out of his grip to beneath his arm. "Let's leave the room in a more civilised way." She couldn't believe she had to be the sensible one. Normally, that was the role of anyone else. Still being sensible, she kept the expression on her face serious as she left ballroom with him.

Sadly, he didn't do anything scandalous. He sat her down on a row of empty chairs in the hallway outside and sat beside her. "I found the girls' mother," he said, in a casual voice.

She turned, delighted, and clasped both her hands around his. "You must be smarter than you look. How on earth did you do that when no one else could?"

He thought for a moment. "I expect I am smarter than I look." He actually looked smug and adorable. "First I spoke to her father, who doubted she would run away and leave her children. Then I investigated."

"Everyone else investigated and found nothing." She kept her gaze fixed on his.

"If she didn't want to leave her children, that meant that she must have been abducted. First, I had to work out who had the means to abduct her. That is, which carriages travelled in that vicinity around the time she disappeared, not that we know the time. We can only have an educated guess. Educated guesses had been done before, without success, because everyone looked in the wrong direction. If she left the bourdaloue shed by the other door, she would have gone through the woods. It would have been easy to get lost, but eventually she would have reached either a road or a farm." He leaned forward and rested his elbows on his parted knees." The story is long and a little complicated."

"I'm not in a hurry." She took note of the length of his explanation. Previously, he had only bothered with short sentences that avoided the letter 's' as much as possible. And he hadn't stuttered a single word. Not only did she love him, she felt proud of him.

He turned his head and looked up at her. "To cut my story shorter, she was either abducted or she had some sort of accident."

"But someone would have found her if she had an accident."

"Not if she hit her head and lost her memory."

She tried to read the adorable smug expression on his face. "Did she?"

He nodded. "Only her memory of who she was and where she was going. Since she had an overnight bag with her, she realised she must have been travelling. Since she didn't wear a satin gown, she decided she was a respectable woman. Anyway, she headed towards the closest village, which she found by spotting the spire of the local church. She walked until she found a well-worn path in the right direction, through fields and pastures. When she reached the village she planned to stand at the post stop, hoping someone might be expecting her. To make the rest of a long complicated s-story shorter, she was directed to a respectable gentleman farmer who was expecting a new housekeeper to arrive." He lifted his shoulders, as if the rest of the story was inevitable.

"So she decided she was his housekeeper."

He nodded. "I heard a longer version of how she found the post stop, but that is mainly right. She still only has vague memories of a family at this stage, but I suspect a jolt will help her. When she sees her daughters, she might remember more."

"Why didn't you bring her back with you?"

"That's a little more complicated to explain."

Daisy tried to look happy about the girl's mother being safe, and she was, but she but she didn't want Mrs. Emerson to be brought back too soon. When she came back, she would take Dawn and Eve, leaving Daisy no excuse to stay with Ash. She would be sent elsewhere since Mama's machinations for Corrine still hadn't lured a marriage proposal for her.

"Let's find a husband for Corrine," she said after some thought.

Ash slapped his knees and laughed. And laughed. "That's the last thing I thought you would say."

"I think I should stay with you a bit longer, don't you?"

He stared at her and slowly nodded.

"If Mrs. Emerson takes her daughters, I don't have a place in your household. I will be sent to stay with some obscure relative, instead. However, if Corrine finds a husband, I can go back to Mama and finally have a season in London." She looked everywhere but at his eyes.

He nodded as if he suddenly understood. "But, I'm going to need you to help Mrs. Emerson with the girls. It may take some time for her to get on her feet. I think we should bring her back to live with us until she does. When the time is right, I will have my lawyer work out a settlement for her. Since it was lack of income that caused her to leave, we must see to that."

Daisy swallowed. He said 'we.' If he meant his mother and him, she didn't mind, for he still held Daisy's hands. "Should we care if Corinne doesn't find a husband?"

"I don't care. It's up to you if you care, but I'm quite sure she will find one without any help. She's pretty and compliant. She would make the perfect wife for someone."

Daisy clamped her lips together and thought about all of Corinne's faults. For one reason or another, she didn't bring any up. "But not you?"

The edges of his mouth curved. "Not me. I prefer scruffy pests who can't even spell 'compliant.'"

"C-o-m-p-l-i-m-e-n-t." She blinked innocently.

With a full-blown grin, he stood and offered his hand, which she took. One moment she was in the corridor and within the next few steps, she was swung into the alcove at the end. Ash removed the curtain sash and hid them both from view.

For a moment she heard nothing but the pounding of her heart. Then she lifted her gaze and saw Ash looking at her with a soft expression on his face.

"May I?" he said stepping closer.

She couldn't answer because she didn't know what she would be permitting. Within a second, he placed his hands on her hips and pulled her right up against his body. She expanded her lungs with a huge breath of shock. Her hands landed on his upper chest and she stood stock-still staring into his eyes. Her heart pounded so hard that her chest hurt. She tried to ease out a breath. If she looked too shocked, he might let go of her and that was the last thing she wanted.

Finally she managed to breathe, and she met his gaze. The man had the audacity to smile at her as if awaiting a response. For the first time in her life, she was determined not to speak first. Feeling rather awkward, for she had never been so close to a man before, she couldn't decide where to put her hands. With a tightening of her shoulders, she placed her fingers lightly on his upper arms. He leaned down and his lips touched hers lightly.

But that was enough encouragement for her. She threw her arms around his neck and tried to kiss him on the lips. His intake of horror moved his chest. Now she had totally embarrassed herself, and she would die. However, she had never been known to admit to embarrassment, and she wouldn't now. And then she didn't need to, for his arms tightened around her and he began to show her how an adult male kissed a woman.

He teased at her lips until she chased his kisses, using the flats of her palms on his cheeks to keep him still. "Daisy," he said between breaths. "You must stop this."

"I can't," she whispered. "You have to."

"I will, but not right at the moment." With that, he gave her a full kiss that lasted all of twenty seconds. Then his arms fell to his sides and he stepped back. He bowed to her as if conceding defeat to the winner.

"If that is an apology, I will hit you," she said in a threatening voice. She didn't want to be the sort of female who could be left blushing and stammering, hoping her swain reciprocated her feelings.

"I never apologise for kissing women." He took her one of her hands in his, and then wrapped her fingers over his bent elbow. "Now, we must return to the ballroom. More than one person saw us leave and I don't plan to cause a scandal with you."

She considered pulling back on his arm, but his arrogance wouldn't let her win. Since he was stronger than she, she marched back into the ballroom with her head held high. Then she spent the rest of the evening wondering why he had taken her into the alcove. Perhaps he thought a kiss from him would be a reward.

Ashford wished he hadn't given in to his urge to kiss the confounded pest. At his age, he should know better than to play with innocents. To show Daisy that kissing her didn't mean a thing to him, for the next few hours, he took up with his usual flirts, most of whom he'd gone past the flirting stage years ago. However, he had no rational thoughts about any of them. Now he'd met Daisy, only one woman would do for him.

He wondered if he could offer for her without being sent packing by her parents, who could probably find someone more suitable with more money and less years. Then he remembered he was now an earl. A title had worth, and would possibly counteract his age. His reputation couldn't stand a close scrutiny, but whose could? Perhaps he wasn't as bad a catch as he had thought. At least he knew how to pleasure a woman. If she wanted him . . . but he wasn't sure she did. She could have been experimenting with her charms, as young ladies were wont to do. He looked across the ballroom at her.

She appeared to be having a rare old time, flirting with all and sundry. He watched her from the sidelines for a while, until he realised that he could spark a reaction from her by asking her sister to waltz. A smile curved his lips as he wandered over to the demure widow. He wasn't the only man with the same thought. Jeremy Hastings stared down at her with a soft expression on his face. If he had feelings for the dashed woman, now was the time to act. A bit of competition might spur him on.

Ashford almost pushed Hastings aside in his rush to steal the next dance. He offered Lady Standing his best smile. "Your sister tells me you are lighter on a man's feet than she is."

Lady Standing stared at him with shock in her eyes. Clearly she didn't share her sister's sense of the ridiculous. "I'm surprised she admitted that, finally."

"I'm here to check the veracity of her words. In other words, may I have the honour of your hand in the quadrille?"

She glanced at Jeremy, her expression a challenge. "Certainly, my lord. I would be delighted."

Jeremy shot him a hurt look. "I was just about to ask her."

"*Just about* is too slow, Hastings. If you want a woman, you have to learn to be much faster." He held out his hand to the not very fast widow, who would suit the not very fast Hastings.

She rose to her feet, rested her hand on his elbow and stood with him during the last moments of the country dance, before she took the floor with him. He searched the room with his gaze, hoping Daisy spotted him with her sister. This would teach her not to melt into the arms of an unsuspecting man in an alcove and then insist on kissing him. Although her idea to marry-off her sister as soon as possible was sound, he would not consider the idea of her going through a season looking for a suitable husband. He'd almost come to terms with being 'suitable' himself after years of being only lover material.

Aside from that, the children loved their mother and shouldn't be kept from them a moment longer than necessary. He wanted to reunite them with their mother within days, not years. But most of all, he wanted Daisy as his wife. He wanted her in his bed as soon as possible, before he took the liberty throwing her onto the nearest flat surface and covering her in his desperate kisses.

The interminable dance finally ended. He took Lady Standing back to her mother's spot, where Hastings still lurked with his arms crossed over his chest and his chin nobly raised. Best of all, Daisy sat beside her mother, her expression thunderous. With one single dance, he had infuriated everyone. For the first time in his life, he hadn't accommodated anyone but himself. In a single step he had moved a thousand paces ahead.

"Did Miss Gerard tell you I found the children's mother?" he said companionably to Lady Gerard.

Lady Gerard shook her head. "She has barely spoken for the past twenty minutes. The music is very loud, you know, and her voice would have been hard to hear." She smiled carefully at her second daughter, who appeared to be on the verge of storming out of the room.

"Mrs. Emerson should be back soon to take charge of her daughters. In the meantime, we still need Miss Gerard, if you don't mind leaving her with us a little longer."

Daisy eyed him sideways, still not speaking.

Her mother said, "I can spare her to you for a few more weeks." She glanced at her older daughter who had her face turned away from Hastings.

If Ashbury could get these two together, his life would stop going sideways and he could ask for Daisy's hand. In the meantime, he was prepared to take whatever she offered, in the full knowledge that he would be marrying her, regardless.

Daisy had the best and the worst night in her life. She'd been kissed and rejected all in the space of two minutes. She'd never been faint of heart but her body hurt all over. That night, she crawled into her bed in the Ashford town-house, none the wiser about why the men she preferred always let her down. From now on, she would concentrate on the girls and how to prepare them for a mother who didn't remember them.

Bleary and disheartened the next morning, she trailed into the nursery room, faking an enormous smile. "Good morning, my best girls. If you can get washed and dressed quickly, I'll take you downstairs to have breakfast with my lord and Mrs. Toddington."

Her best girls grinned with delight. Dawn began to busily wash herself and then she helped Eve, while Daisy cracked the gowns of each in the air to remove some of the resting wrinkles. She had done this to her own gown and had dressed her own hair, seeing no point in going to any lengths for Ash now that he had played with her and laughed at her gullibility.

Within five minutes, she marched into the breakfast room with her trail of small girls behind. Mrs. Toddington smiled at everyone. Ash raised his head, looking beautiful and untouchable. If she didn't love him, she would hate him for this alone. But Ash would never know that she had been irrevocably hurt by his rejection of her. "Good morning," she said in bright voice.

Two adult voices echoed her sentiment, one meaning the words and the other staring at her as if she had lost her marbles. Ash said, "How lovely to see my most favourite young ladies for breakfast. While you are eating, I will share my good news with you."

Her eyes widened in surprise. "With me too?"

"Naturally. That is, if you think you are one of my favourite ladies." Ash's face expressed nothing but good humour. "I think every female at this table this morning is one of my favourite ladies, young or ..." He saw the trap before he went any farther. His mother eyed him narrowly. "Young or grown up."

"Good save, dear," his mother said. "What is the news?"

"I found Dawn and Eve's mother."

Three pairs of eyes widened. One little girl slid off her chair, rounded the table and grabbed Ash by his jacket front. "Mummy!" Dawn said excitedly tugging on the fabric. "Where is she?

"She'll be here in a day or two. I'll send the carriage for her, tomorrow. We must get a room ready for her," he said to his mother, while he tried to peel Dawn's fingers off his perfectly cut jacket.

"We'll have to put her in guest room for the time being. When we go back to the country she can have a whole floor with the girls."

"I doubt it will come to that."

"What do you mean?" his mother said, staring at Ash.

"We'll speak about this later." He eyed the children, indicating that whatever he said wasn't mean for young ears. "Daisy, would you accompany me for a drive in the park?"

Daisy choked on a sip of tea. "Have you run out of merry widows?" she said, after her breath returned.

"I have an interminable supply, but today I want you."

She hated the way he stole her breath every time he glanced at her. If he wanted her, it would never be the way she wanted to be wanted. He had a distasteful task for her perform and wanted to sugar the request. "I'm sorry." She jutted her jaw. "I'm engaged otherwise."

"What wise?"

"I need to go over to my parent's house and annoy Corrine for a while. She is looking too smug lately, and I must put a stop to that."

He and his mother glanced at each other, each in a different stage of smiling. She had a naughty smile and he had smug one. His mother said, "I'm going to be so upset if she has a proposal and leaves the scene too soon."

Ash raised his gaze heavenwards. "Be ready in five minutes," he said to Daisy in an autocratic voice.

She glanced at him in surprise. He stared back with a steely gaze. Her breath caught. She had never seen him like this before. Her pulse began to panic and she had the idea that if she didn't do as he said, he would pick her up and throw her into his curricle.

Accordingly, in five minutes, she stood on the front step, her bonnet crushed on her head, her gloves mid mast, and her reticule strings twisted around her fingers.

Chapter Twelve

"This will be my first promenade in the park." Settling precariously on the forward seat of the curricle with Ash, Daisy offered him a shaky smile. "I'm feeling quite the society lady now." She glanced at the trail of clouds stretched over the pale blue sky behind him.

"Do you know what the word 'promenade' means?"

She blinked at him. "Of course I do."

"Then you would know it is related to walking."

She carefully arranged her skirts over her knees. Being accompanied by the most handsome lord in London meant she had to live up to him. Only the most stylish of ladies could expect his escort. The others could only live in hope. "Your horses are walking, aren't they?"

"Good point." His horses neatly clipped around the first corner. "I wanted to speak to you alone where no one can overhear or interrupt."

Her heart sank and her mouth dried. "Tell me now if it's bad news."

"I'm hoping you don't think it's bad."

"Tell me *right now*. Let me judge." She turned and, without a second thought, clutched at his jacket sleeve.

He concentrated on the road ahead, his hands steadying his horses to take the next turn. "A dusty street filled with busy passers-by is not an appropriate setting for the words I need to say. I have chosen Green Park."

She examined the serious expression on his face. The tightening of his jaw said he wouldn't change his mind. Growing more nervous by the second, she watched as his curricle neatly took the entrance into the park. The horses clipped over a dusty path through to the shady trees in the centre. Ash pulled up the curricle, and then he swivelled around and glanced at his groom. Her seat sprang higher when the man leapt off and wandered over to a group of spindly bushes.

"Now we have a little privacy."

A thousand drums set up a competition in her chest. If the reason why he wanted to be alone with her meant that he simply wanted to be alone with her, she would take that as a positive. Nothing awful had ever happened when he was alone with her. He had kissed her once. She hoped he wouldn't kiss her again, or she might make a fool of herself and grab hold of him and never let him go.

He wound his reins around the brake handle and turned to her, staring at her in silence for far too long. Finally, he said, the words she thought she would never hear from anyone. "I love you, Daisy."

Nothing could have prepared her for this. She couldn't have said a word if her life depended on her speaking. She sat, her eyes fixed on his, dragging in one breath after another. Not a single smart word came to her mind. Her throat had totally dried up.

"As a former stutterer, I have no fluent words prepared for my first and only proposal." He carefully picked up her right hand and held her fingers with his, concentrating on her palm. "You are my everything. Now that I have met you, I doubt I can live without you. Will you take my heart with my hand?" He raised his gaze to hers.

The most beautiful man in the world couldn't possibly want to marry a scruffy pest like her. She tried to find a light quip and or an amused smile. Neither happened. She swallowed. "If you meant that, you would have asked my parents first." Her breath eased out shakily.

"I wanted to propose to you first. If I asked your parents, they would take you back, and you would leave my house and I want you too much to lose you at this time."

"But …"

He held up a stopping hand. "Any more objections and I'll be bound to stutter. Yes or no?"

"Yes, of course." She almost sounded panicked, but his suggestion that her parents would grab her back told her that he knew them as well as she did.

They would want her wrapped and packaged to go to a husband. They would want to organise every function known to society to show that same society that daughter number two had attracted a man with a title. No one expected an awkward second daughter like her to do better than a wealthy gentleman. Daughter number one was a different matter. Corrine had always been expected to shine, and Daisy had always been expected to grab up the glittery beads that fell off her sister's gowns.

Then Ash's words really sunk in. He loved her and wanted to marry her. "You love me?" Her gaze fixed on his.

"How else could I have put up with your cheery morning remarks and your dashed interference in my life?"

"That doesn't sound at all romantic. It isn't how I expected to be proposed to."

"Of course it is. If I got down on one knee, you would push me over. That's the sort of woman you are." A smile tugged at his lips. "Incredible." He said these last words while he put his arm around her shoulder and slowly moved her closer to him. "Yes or no?"

"No. I wouldn't push you over. I would give you a hand up," she said in huffy-puffy voice. She had no idea what she was talking about. After the word 'love,' she had lost track of the whole conversation.

"Was that a 'yes'?"

"Yes, of course, but you will have to ask my parents as well," she said in a panicked voice. She still couldn't believe she had heard what she had heard.

"I will, but I can't wait to kiss you any longer." Then he dragged her over to him and wrapped both of his arms around her.

After a few minutes of listening to his beating heart, she stared up at him. He smiled down at her and softly placed his mouth on hers. In her mind, she was a 'fast' girl, and her body agreed with her mind. A gentle press of lips didn't satisfy her at all. She threw her arms around his neck and kissed him back. The curricle jolted. His hands moved quickly to grab up the reins again, but he kept kissing her. She could tell he had lost concentration on one task, and that was kissing her, for he pulled back a little.

"My horses are trying to tell me that this is not the right place for making love to you."

She tried to look like an innocent little flower but she had a very good idea, although no first hand experience, of what 'making love' entailed. "Don't you have to marry me first?"

He leaned back and examined her expression. "Conventionally, yes. But, in reality, no. But I will wait until marriage if that's what you want."

"I need to think."

"No, you don't. Just imagine what Corrine would do in this situation and do the opposite."

She made a pretence of thinking. "Where is the right place to make love to me?"

"In my bedroom."

"What about your mother?"

"I don't think she needs to participate. My suite is nowhere near hers, and my deeds are not her responsibility."

"But she is supposed to be my chaperone."

He gave a loud and impatient sigh. "Well, then, I will need to speak to your parents and ask for your hand, and delay the love making."

She grabbed his sleeve. "If you do, I will be trundled from one dressmaker to the next, and sent around to all our relatives to share my good news. You will get my parents' permission, but I would hardly ever see you. Are you sure you want to delay the love making?"

He stared at her with raised eyebrows. A slow smile formed on his lips.

She concentrated on her folded fingers for a while, in no

doubt that she wanted him, and not doubting he wanted her. Finally, she heaved a fake impatient sigh. "Well then, I suppose we'll have to make love first."

"Morning, noon, and night, my dearest love." With that, he beckoned his groom who came rushing over. "But I will speak to your parents fairly soon."

Ashbury longed to make love to Daisy, but the moment he began to hurry her into the hallway of his townhouse, he heard his name called. His mother stood at the top of the stairway. He stopped and glared at her.

She glanced from him to Daisy. Her eyes widened. Her lips opened, and then closed. "I have decided to go out most of the day. When I get back, I will speak to you." Without another word, she headed for her bedroom. Apparently, his face said everything.

He turned to Daisy who was latched to his arm. "You are irrevocably compromised now."

The hints of a smile formed on her lips. "So are you. Now you are definitely going to have to marry me."

His mouth quirked into a rueful grin. "I'll remember that, you can be sure. I have changed my mind about compromising you. I think you ought to go wherever my mother is going and go with her. Don't wait up for me."

Daisy clung to his arm. "Don't you dare leave me now that you have made me look like a wicked woman."

"If you leave with my mother, you won't be a wicked woman."

He peeled her fingers off his arm and strode back

outside. From there, he went to see a second cousin who also happened to be a bishop. He needed to be polite for a while, and take a glass of wine, which kept him longer than he had planned, and then he chased the trail of Daisy's mother for about an hour until he found her.

Dusk had begun to descend before he arrived back home, a satisfied man.

Two little girls bounced down the stairs to greet him. "Mummy's here," Dawn said excitedly. Her smile reached from ear to ear. Before he had time to digest her words, without a word of warning, she made a great leap into his arms.

He reeled backwards, catching her and balancing her on his forearm. Steadying them both, he tried to understand why on earth the fates conspired against him, making him take one step forward and the next back, literally in this case. His mother must have heard him come in, for she opened the drawing room door and beckoned him in. "Mummy's here?" he asked her, with one little girl on his hip and the other clinging to his coat tail.

"She's resting, dear. We'll leave her for the time being."

Then Daisy rushed into the room. "My little devils escaped when they heard you arrive. It's way past their bed time."

He managed to smile at her before he had his head turned by Dawn's tiny hands on his cheeks. Apparently he was supposed to be looking at her.

"Mummy said we are going to live with her."

Since he hadn't found a place for Mrs. Emerson yet, he nodded without conviction. "She can live with you in the country house as soon as she is well enough."

Daisy held out both her hands and each little girl took one, obediently. "I'll take you both back to your bedroom now. It's well past your bedtime."

As the chattering group left the room, Ash turned to his mother. "I wasn't expecting Mrs. Emerson so soon. Did she say why she came today?"

"Apparently she has remembered more about her children and desperately wanted to see them. I know how she feels. I would like to see my son occasionally, but I'm not expecting to live with him much longer." His mother tried to look mournful, but the twinkle in her eyes let her down.

"As to that," he said, sitting down with her. "As you've rightly guessed, I asked Daisy to marry me. I have permission from her family and I will be marrying her tomorrow."

"I know you love her, and rightly so, for she is the most darling girl—but I don't think she knows about the wedding, dear," she said without a stir of a single hair on her head. "She has all sorts of plans for tomorrow."

"I'll overturn them all. Her parents seem to think that the sooner she is wed, the better for all. I, of course, agree." He tried to sound confident, but his day had gone to hell and back. He had planned to be sleeping with woman he loved tonight and that plan had been overturned, like so many of his plans, by his houseful of females.

Finally, Daisy came back, her hair looking like a bird's nest, but she had a huge smile on her face. "I didn't know that two happy children could be so exhausting. I don't think we should have children right away, Ash." She glanced at his mother. "I suspect he has told you that we plan to marry."

His mother nodded. "I've been waiting for that

announcement for weeks. I'm so glad for both of you. Do you mind if I give you a sound kissing?"

Daisy's face dimpled. She moved over to his mother and grabbed up her hands. "I'm so glad that you approve." With that, she leaned down and accepted a kiss placed on each of her cheeks. "I hope my parents will be as easy to deal with as you."

Ashbury smiled. "They said they are delighted to get rid of you, and will be at the Bishop's townhouse at ten tomorrow morning, to watch the event."

"Tomorrow?" Her eyes widened.

He nodded.

She examined the expression on his face, before an over-done fluttering of her eyelashes. "Oh, but what if I want a huge society wedding?"

"I can't arrange one for at least a month. Do you want to wait that long?"

"Let me think." Daisy folded her arms across her chest and lifted one finger to her cheek, imitating a person thinking.

His mother said, "I think I'll have a tray sent up to my room. You two clearly have much to discuss. Let me know what the plan is later."

He stood watching Daisy, who offered him a glance of complicity as his mother left the room.

"Finally." She lowered herself into an armchair. "This day has been the most exhausting day of my life."

He read her expression easily, and nodded wryly. "I suppose you ought to have a quiet night, so that you can be well rested before the wedding."

"Good idea," she said wearily. "Tomorrow is bound to be worse."

"Says the lucky woman who is about to marry the man of her dreams." He strolled over to her and took her hand. "I love you, Daisy. Tomorrow is the start of the best days of our lives."

She sat up, her expression softening as she stared at him. His heart gave a loud thump. He had never experienced this sort of love for a woman. He thought he had loved Anna, but his feelings for her had faded into a pleasant memory. Daisy was all he could see now. Her ridiculous sense of humour kept him smiling on dull days and made good days even better. He couldn't help himself from gathering her up in his arms.

She smiled at him tremulously. Her hand settled on the back of his neck and her gaze centred on his mouth. Time stood still while he lowered his head and settled his lips on hers. Her lovely mouth softened as he pressed a gentle kiss on her waiting mouth. He started gently, but her chin lifted to take more from him. Although he thought he could kiss her for hours, each kiss became more urgent. A gentleman would stop at this point and wait until tomorrow. A lady would expect nothing less. However, his delicious Daisy always expected the most she could have.

Reluctantly, he lifted his head. "No more of this until you are wed, young lady."

"Are you suddenly my guardian?" she asked in her huffy-puffy voice, which meant she had taken his measure.

"I'm the man about whom guardians would warn a nice young lady."

"Fortunately, you are not speaking to a nice young lady.

You are speaking to a spinster who has been left on the shelf forever and is hungry for man who needs to come with a warning flag." She grabbed him by the hair on the back of his head and lifted her face to accept more of his kisses.

Being a gentleman, he obliged with an urgent kiss. Being a man, he lifted her into his arms and instantly headed for the stairs.

"Put me down. You'll never be able to carry a healthy woman up two flights of stairs."

"I see that as a challenge, as any man would." He faked staggering for the first three steps, causing her to hold him tighter. Smug about reaching his aim, he hurried up to the landing. A movement higher up caught his eye. He stopped, noting Mrs. Emerson standing at the top of the staircase, gazing at him. "Good evening," he said courteously, warning the clinging Daisy that they weren't alone.

Daisy glanced up. "I thought you were sleeping."

Mrs. Emerson said, "I'm sorry to disturb you. What I have to say will wait until the morning." She turned to leave.

Ash reached the top, holding his bundle of joy. Then he put her down, right beside Mrs. Emerson. "I hope your ankle recovers before the wedding," he said to Daisy in a dismissive voice. Then he bowed politely at the widow. "Now would be a more convenient time." He indicated the downstairs to Mrs. Emerson, and the bedroom wing to Daisy. Apparently, the night he had hoped for would have to wait for yet another day.

He hastened back to his guest and guided her into his study, seating her in the comfortable chair near the window.

The sun had lowered to tree top height and the last of the daylight surrounded her head. "Are you comfortable?"

"Yes, sir." For a moment she tangled her fingers together and then she focussed on his face. Her long breath lifted her shoulders. "I remember more and more each time I'm with the girls. Some of the details after hitting my head seem to be gone forever, but I remember almost everything about my previous life. The thing is ..."

He waited.

"I have a new life now and hope to marry again. Mr. Feathers asked for my hand." Her eyes met his.

He tried to hide his apprehension with a surprised glance. If she wanted to desert her daughters, he would accept them, but he knew they loved her and wanted to be with her. But, more than likely, the farmer wouldn't want to be saddled with another man's children. "And ..." he asked with a tilt of his eyebrows.

"And the girls want to live with me."

"Are they an impediment to your marriage?" He smiled as he said the words, so that she would feel she could speak the truth.

She shook her head. "Mr. Feathers is a good man. He hopes you will allow me to keep them."

His shoulders relaxed and his chest emptied with a sight of relief. He offered her a formal bow. "Although I have charge of Dawn and Eve at the moment, I didn't inherit their guardianship from my uncle. They belong to you and you alone. Although I have enjoyed borrowing your daughters for a while, they miss their mother badly."

Tears slowly ran down Mrs. Emerson's cheeks. He stepped forward with a handkerchief and a spare shoulder to cry on. When her sobs finally ceased, he dabbed at the trail until she took over and noisily blew her nose. She offered him a shaky smile and took a deep breath. "I'll accompany the girls to your wedding, sir, and then I'll take them back to the farm with me. I hope you will do me the honour of attending my wedding next month."

"I would be delighted to attend." After she left for her room, he rubbed the back of his neck, trying to ease his tension. His own wedding couldn't happen quickly enough, but the bedding would have to wait. Daisy would have gone to sleep long since.

With nothing but the next morning's event in mind, he trudged up the stairs to his rooms again. As he closed the door, he thought about calling for his valet. His hand reached out for the bell pull when a voice said, "Don't you dare."

He swivelled around to see Daisy in his bed, sitting comfortably against his pillows, her hair brushed out for the night, and her face aglow with a mischievous smile. His chest expanded with love. "How good to see you here," he said inanely as he walked over to her.

She grabbed his hands and pulled him down to sit at her side. "I thought I should practice the wedding night, so that I don't make a mistake on the most important night of my life."

"Mine too," he said as he leaned across her and gently kissed her on the mouth. "But I don't want you to look tired on the most important day of your life."

"Are you thinking of keeping me up late?"

He gave a wry smile. "I need a rest as much as you do."

Her expression changed to one of complete understanding. "I know I don't want to look haggard at my own wedding, but I want to share your bed tonight. I have no one else to confide in. If I were at home, I would probably sleep with Corrine on this night of nights."

"I know I will be poor substitute for Corrine, but you are welcome to share my bed tonight." He said this without blinking, knowing that he wouldn't take advantage her if she cared to stay.

In answer, she pulled aside the bed quilt, and sat up with her arms around her knees as if awaiting him to strip. He made a quick decision. She would have to see his body at sometime therefore he turned toward his dressing room and undressed. He returned wearing his blue silk dressing robe. By this time she no longer sat in the middle but to the left side, leaving him a generous space. He blew out the candle that normally resided on the table, leaving the room in semi darkness. After sliding down the bed, he groped around and found her hand, which he held in his. "Is this what Corrine would do?"

He heard a sound like a giggle. "We would talk until one of us became bored and stopped."

"What would you like to talk about?"

"Nothing."

He closed his eyes. "We can sleep then. Tomorrow will be exhausting." The bed quilt moved as she did. Opening his eyes a crack, he saw the outline of one shoulder, meaning she had turned toward him. He let go of her hand so that he could rest his other hand on her hip. She made a sound of contentment, and moved right into him.

He drew a deep breath, remaining perfectly still, hoping she didn't mean to test his control. Her wispy hair tickled his nose and he moved his face upwards, which meant her head rested beneath his chin. She snuggled even closer. He'd never held a woman until she slept in his whole life. He usually fell asleep first and left the morning-after conversations until a reasonable hour. The idea of spending the night with his own woman and having breakfast with her somehow hit him in the heart.

He rested his cheek on her head, his love for her consuming him, trying not to worry about how to handle a virgin. However, his very own virgin began to snuggle even closer. She wriggled her pelvis right into him. Naturally, his body responded, but of course he had control of his actions. Being erect didn't mean he had to act on his urges, though his body thought otherwise. Nevertheless he remained in the same position, holding her close and breathing into her hair. Then she slid her hand to his hip.

"Go to sleep or I will deliver you wrapped in a quilt to your own room."

"If I were your concubine, I would be delivered to you wrapped in a quilt."

Realising she had a better education than most young ladies, he said, "Daisy, my darling, we need sleep. Tomorrow will be exhausting for both of us."

"I know. I'm trying to keep my hands off you, but your body is so beautiful that I just want to touch you."

"I find it hard to argue with that but we can be intimate with a view to sleeping."

She laughed softly. "I love you, Ash," she whispered into his ear.

He grabbed her tightly and held her close to his heart. Being loved by this wilful, adorable pest was the greatest achievement of his life. He had never imagined being at all interested in a woman so much younger than he, but her brightness and willingness to help anyone had changed his lonely life. She remained in his arms until she fell asleep. He finally closed his eyes when dawn hadn't yet emerged over the horizon. Moving her arm that sat across his chest, he prepared to climb out bed and escort her back to her room before the maids began to stir.

She grabbed him. "Kiss me before I go," she said in a far from sleepy voice.

"How long have you been awake?"

"Long enough to have seen you sleeping soundly. I doubt I could marry a man who snored, and fortunately you don't."

"I'm glad to hear that."

She planted a kiss on his lips while she grabbed him by the collar of his dressing robe. Never had he ever been so guilelessly assaulted. He wanted to laugh but instead he kissed her with a barely restrained passion. His body overreacted and he wanted her beneath him. With only a few hours to wait until wedding her, he thought going too far would be a reckless move. Therefore he breathed deeply and satisfied himself with light kisses.

Apparently light kisses didn't satisfy her one bit. She set her hands beneath his dressing robe and began to smooth the skin of his chest. His heart began to bump and his skin heated. His mouth fastened on hers, and he rolled her over to her back. With a magnificent feat of strength, he managed not to part her legs for his body to rest there. He tried his best to give her a goodbye kiss, but her lips clung to his.

He didn't want frighten her off before he had the ring on her finger. So said his befuddled mind. His body had other ideas. Instead of fighting her off, he had to fight his own desires. To regain control of her and himself, he rolled to one side, taking her with him, leaving her facing him. "I love you."

"I love you too," she said, in a whispery voice.

"I also want to love your body."

He felt her draw breath. "Are you asking for my permission?"

"If the answer is 'no' you may return to your own room."

She answered by throwing her arms around his neck. "I will leave before morning but until then, I want my body loved."

Although he was in no doubt that she had no idea what she had asked for, he began by scooping his hands under her arms and bringing them forward to cup her breasts. His thumbs moved to her nipples, clearly felt over her night-gown. She shivered. He continued until she began to relax in his arms. He pressed his mouth to hers and tested her desire for him.

One of her hands lifted to the back of his head while she opened her lips to him. In the middle of a desperate kiss, she rolled on top of him. He hadn't expected anything quite so forward, but she was his Daisy, his indomitable Daisy, and she would take whatever she wanted. His own lips smiled as he responded with more desperation than he had planned. He rolled her over, changing positions with her. This way he could lie between her legs and simulate what might happen on the wedding night.

She seemed unprepared when his uncontrollable erection pressed so avidly at her entrance that the separating material of her nightgown appeared to have dissolved. She wriggled against him greedily while his kisses ran all over her face and down to her arching neck. By this stage his skin was hot enough to melt a block of ice in two seconds. He'd thought he would be the seducer and she would be the seduced, but she had levelled him by her response. He longed to lift her nightgown and enter her but he knew that would be the end of him. Instead, he ran his hand up the inside of her leg and found her pleasure spot.

She gave a sharp intake of breath and her knees stiffened. "Will this hurt?"

"No. This is how women find the greatest pleasure. Some women find it before marriage and some never do."

She lay still waiting for his next move. He began gently stroking her until her body insisted on him rolling her nub between his fingers. She arched with pleasure and grabbed his behind and dug her fingers into him, but he would not take her so soon. Unfortunately, being virginal, she didn't find the ultimate pleasure but he decided she had had enough of this for the night. He began to smooth over her and take down the intensity of his kissing until she and he began to breath at a normal rate.

After that, he held her in his arms for a while, before sitting up beside her. "It's time you left, Miss Gerard. I want to see you looking fresh and bright in the morning and you won't if you stay any longer with me."

She sat bolt upright and swivelled around so that her feet landed on the floor. Her gray shadow left the room without a sound.

Chapter Thirteen

Daisy awoke to a bright morning filled with sunlight, which expressed her mood entirely. Last night with Ash had been beautiful. She couldn't wait to marry him and spend every night in his arms. Her own parents still shared a bed, which Daisy knew was unusual for the gentry. She wanted the same comfortable relationship for herself.

Although she would have liked to be with her family on the morning of her wedding, in almost no time at all, she would see everyone, except for her brother, Bertie, who was touring the continent. However, Mrs. Toddington's help would be more useful than her own mother's, being so stylish herself. Naturally, Daisy wanted to look her best for Ash on her wedding day.

When she had invited herself into Ash's bed last night, she hadn't worried about how she looked. A night candle tended to cast flattering shadows on anyone. Not that Ash needed a scrap of flattery regarding *his* looks. The man had been blessed from the day he was born. She didn't want to be shallow regarding handsome men, but who could help but admire a man whose every angle took a woman's breath. Now she knew his hands could do the same thing to a woman's body.

She knew he'd had mistresses, but she didn't want to think about his previous lovers this morning. Since he hadn't married before, she could be secure in the knowledge that she had beaten them all off. She slid out of bed and rang for a maid. Smithson arrived and warned her that a bath would arrive soon. Knowing that two footmen would be bringing the bath, she donned a dressing robe and sat in the bedroom chair, awaiting the luxury. Within minutes, a bath clattered into the room, trailed by two maids carrying buckets. Apparently everyone had been organised the night before.

She supposed no one knew she had spent the night with Ash, but even if they did, no one gave a sign. After her bath, Smithson helped her with the fastenings on her wedding gown. Mrs. Toddington had found a pale yellow, with a white overlay, and someone to embroider daisies around the hem and neckline. Naturally, a daisy had never been her favourite flower, but today the sight of her own daisies warmed her heart.

Smithson added a few curls around her face to her normal upswept hairdo. "Are the girls ready?" Daisy caught Smithson's critical eyes.

"Their mother is helping them dress. They'll be ready to leave when you do." Smithson carefully placed a white silk bonnet on Daisy's head.

She stared at herself in the mirror for some time, almost not recognising herself. When she had been brought to stay with the Ashford family, she had been scruffy and angry. In the mirror she saw a woman who looked calm, tidy, and breathlessly happy. She didn't mind in the least about not having a debut or a big wedding. All she wanted was Ash.

For some unknown reason, she wasn't supposed to see him before the wedding, but the idea seemed wise because she would throw herself into his arms if he gave her his longing look.

With Smithson ushering her, incase she unravelled somehow, she finally walked into the sitting room. In less than a minute, the girls raced into the room followed by their sweet and gentle mother. After every possible question had been answered, including why she looked so grown-up today – the answer being because today was a very important day – they began to cling to their mother's hands. Daisy loved to see them so possessive and happy to be with the lovely woman. She doubted they cared where they lived as long as she lived with them.

All being right with the world on the best day of her life, she turned to smile at Mrs. Toddington who entered the room looking as elegant as usual with a carefully plain gown in dark blue and the smartest hat Daisy had ever seen, a dark blue with bright emerald green feathers placed perfectly on her head. "Oh, my," she said, glancing at the assembled company. "The smartest dressed ladies of the ton will be accompanying me to my wedding."

Everyone either smiled or laughed, because as usual, the smartest dressed was always Mrs. Toddington.

Without any further ado, three ladies and two small girls piled into Ash's town carriage.

Ashford stood in the sitting room of the house of his cousin, the bishop, with Daisy's close family, which consisted of her parents and her sister. His cousin idly talked about this and that while Ashbury stared at the door. Finally, the butler opened the doors. His mother with Mrs. Emerson, and the two girls entered. He waited for Daisy to enter but instead, her father left the room. He glanced at Lady Gerard but she nodded reassuringly.

His apprehension grew. He hadn't noted the plans, having too much to do on the previous day. Breathing shallowly, he told himself she wouldn't back out after last night, smiled calmly and kept waiting.

Finally, Daisy stood in the doorway with her father. For a woman who had tried to keep him awake all night, she appeared remarkably unflustered. She offered him one of her mischievous smiles and his heart almost bounded out of his chest. He managed a complicit smile. Then she began to walk towards him. Somehow everyone had been arranged so that they stood on either side of an invisible path that led to him. While he watched, his heart thundered, and his breath seemed to drag.

She reached his side and smiled up at him, then at his cousin who stood behind him. The wedding vows began and finished at the final 'I do.' When everyone closed around him, and the thrown rose petals drifted onto the vicar's best Indian rugs, Ashford realised that he was now a married man. He grabbed up Daisy and kissed her on her lips, for a mite too long.

Not wanting to make a spectacle of Daisy, he made

himself step back and put her hand on his arm instead, while everyone showered him with best wishes. Finally, all the courtesies observed, he headed with Daisy to his travelling carriage that had bought him here today. Unbelievably, he hadn't stuttered once. He bundled her in, and stepped in beside her. The carriage creaked into a start and he finally headed for his honeymoon cottage.

Daisy pulled off her gloves, and untied the ribbons of her hat. She heaved a sigh. "All that dressing for a ten-second wedding. Next time I get married, I won't take so much trouble. It was worth it, though. Corrine's eyes almost popped out of head. I could see her envying my gown."

He remained silent for a minute or two, while he thought about his phrasing. Then he leaned over and took her hand in his. "You don't need to compare yourself with your sister any longer. You are perfect just the way you are."

She examined his expression, carefully. "I know I'm a pest and I know how patient you are," she said holding his gaze. "But I've spent years being the lesser sister. The only way I could hold up my head was to make note of her perfection, and do the opposite."

"And at the same time, amuse yourself. Yes, I know that's what you do. But you are you, and she is she." He stared right into her eyes. "And I love you exactly the way you are." When he saw her expression soften, he added with lightness in his heart, "Though, if you want to continue amusing me with your comments about her, go ahead."

She waited for a while, considering, before she hauled in a breath, faking relief. "She wouldn't know what to do with herself if she thought I thought she was perfect."

He leaned his head back and laughed, pulling her into his arms. "Daisy, my darling one, please never change."

For a moment her expression turned serious. She looked into his eyes before she rested her head on his shoulder and moved her hand to his chest. He dipped his head to kiss her. Her arm encircled his neck and she clung tightly to him, moving to sit in his lap. Her mouth pressed urgently against his. His whole body responded, first by heating, then with the inevitable male reaction. He would willingly take her, but not to sate himself. She needed to be readied first. Therefore he kept kissing her, changing the angle, and the depth.

He kissed her lips, her eyes, her forehead, her cheeks, the tips of each ear, and then her lips again. She tasted of ardour and breathlessness, willingness and love. Her skin was petal soft, like her generous heart. Her hands clutched at the back of his jacket.

Her urgency transferred to him and he couldn't stop kissing her. He recalled the phrase 'in the heat of love,' finally knew what the words meant. Love coursed through him. Instead of thinking about tossing her on her back and finishing the act before the first post house, he thought of holding her forevermore, keeping her safe, and being with her for the rest of his life. Instead, he could concentrate on the movements of his hands so that he could pleasure her without overwhelming her. Being careful, he cupped her beautiful breasts in his palms.

She stiffened a little but he simply weighed her bounty without trying to further stimulate her, thinking a young virgin needed more than careful handling. He gentled his kisses, awaiting her reaction. She seemed to have grown a little breathless but continued kissing him. After a while, she slid her hand under his jacket and around to his back.

She kissed him. Beneath her lips, his curled into a smile. He loved the way she experimented with him. Unfortunately, he didn't have full control of his reactions. He opened his eyes and noted the length of her fine eyelashes and how they tickled across her cheeks. His breath shortened and her urgency was replaced by his, the only difference being that he knew what would happen next, and she didn't. He knew he would do nothing at all but hold her and attempt to keep the kissing under his control.

Perhaps he didn't express this decision clearly enough, for the kiss grew more insistent, but not on her part. He pulled back to change the position of his mouth, quite a number of times. His skin heated and his hands began to roam a distance away from her back. He found her breasts again and her perky little nipples, which he smoothed across with his palms, before scooping her up in his arms.

"Put me down," she said in breathless voice. "You may not have noticed, but we are in a travelling carriage."

"No one could be more aware of that." He grabbed her lips with his again, and then again. Somehow he had lowered her on her back and manoeuvred himself on top of her.

She lifted her knees either side of him. "I think we should stop this, don't you?" Then she wriggled against him.

He wondered if she had had more experience than he had imagined, but now was not the time to care about any such thing. Mainly, because he didn't care. He hadn't been seeking a virgin bride and whatever had happened in her life before him only mattered as much as anything that had happened in his life before her. "I don't think we should stop this, but rather, we should go no further. Not because I don't want to, but because as soon as we reach the next toll gate, we could be embarrassed."

With that, she sat up and put her hand to her hair. Her cheeks appeared lightly flushed, a sight that he could hardly believe. He had never thought Daisy would be embarrassed about anything.

"Well, you are wrong. I can always be embarrassed about messy hair."

"When I first met you, you weren't the slightest embarrassed about your hair."

"That's before I knew better. Now I know how my hair should be done, I want to keep up my standards."

"I'm insanely in love with you, Daisy," he said quietly as he pulled her back into his arms. He rested his face on her messy hair. "You're never at a loss."

"I adore you because you understand whatever I say. You don't look shocked or puzzled or patronising. You look gorgeous every single minute of your life."

"I hope you aren't marrying me because of the way I look." She raised her chin.

"Plenty of men marry women because of the way they look."

"I doubt it happens as much as you think. When you love, you see the inner person that other people can't see. You are just as beautiful on the inside as you are on the outside."

He placed a thoughtful kiss on her forehead. Although he had worried about the age difference, he now felt at ease.

Despite her age, she had far more sense than many a person twice her age.

The carriage slowed. Apparently the tollgate had been reached. Within another half hour, they would reach the inn he had booked for the night.

Daisy enjoyed wandering around the countryside with her brand new husband, who had borrowed a sulky from the innkeeper. He planned to see the husbandry on all the local farms, in case anyone had an idea he could use. Apparently, having his new bride with him made his entry easier. He introduced her and himself to everyone he wanted to interview, his word for grabbing whatever gossip he could. Most of the local farmers hadn't met him yet, since they didn't live in his immediate vicinity, but all had heard his name mentioned.

Daisy's role appeared to be asking the farmers' wives about their children, and recipes for anything she could think of. Strangely enough, she really enjoyed the afternoon, going out-and-about with her new husband. Her pride in him kept a smile on her face. She didn't mind sharing him with others during the daylight, for she knew she would have him to herself that night. Although she tried not to be apprehensive, she had enough pride to know that a man with plenty of experience in the bedroom wouldn't want his new young wife to act the timid virgin. He would want a woman who was willing to share her love with him.

Finally, dusk began to settle. Ash drove the sulky back

to the inn as the distant trees shivered in the cool breeze. A substantial meal had been prepared by the innkeeper for his noble guests. Daisy managed a quick tidy up of her hair, and brushed down her travelling gown instead of changing for dinner, although she could have called for a maid to help her.

She and her new husband ate a leisurely meal, while intermittently staring at each other, she trying not to smile like a besotted new bride, and he with an expression of tenderness in his eyes. She couldn't wait to hold him and she assumed that showed, for he made quick work of the roast and the following apple pie, accompanied with a red wine.

Finally the meal finished, he thanked the host and grabbed Daisy's hand and hurried her up the stairs. "Are you in a rush, my lord?" she asked in an innocent voice, laughing inside.

His answer was to hold the bedroom door open for her to enter. "Tonight, I shall be your maid."

"Should I be your valet?"

"If you please, my lady."

He had her down to her petticoats before she was allowed remove his jacket, his cravat, and his shirt. For the first time, she had glimpse of his chest. She couldn't take her eyes off him. He had a build like a labourer, all hard muscle. Her breath eased out. She hadn't even touched his bare skin, before her insides had begun to quiver. But she wanted all of him, not simply glimpses of a man who managed, by being sometimes adorable, sometimes relaxed, and very often humorous, to appeal to her weaknesses. Making love to him would be more than an experience.

Being with him could make an ordinary woman into a wanton, even if only for a short time.

He sat on her bed and scooped off his shoes. Her heart skittered. She wanted him to be slow and patient. She suppressed the urge to protest as he spun her around and unlaced her petticoat. The silk fabric pooled around her on the floor. Whatever eventuated, she'd made a commitment to him forevermore. A movement on the opposite wall caught her eye, a reflection of him and her in the small mirror hanging on the window wall. She saw his face, showing neither determination nor satisfaction. With his gaze lowered to her shoulders, where his hands caressed her, he looked overcome, as if he didn't know what to do next.

She watched a partially naked woman in a white cotton chemise standing proud and tall while the gloriously hand-some man behind her hesitated. Power had been given back to her, and understanding. For once, he seemed less certain than she did.

He lifted his head and saw her watching him. His breath steadied. "This underwear of yours is in the way. Tonight I want you naked in my bed." His lips brushed over the side of her neck as he slipped her lace straps down her arms.

Her skin heated. A flare of desire licked through her body as he bared her breasts. She looked wanton in the mirror, but he looked desirous. His hands cupped her breasts, shaping them to his palms.

Then he, too, watched their reflection, his thumbs and fingers beginning an exciting slide around her nipples, a smoothing forward to the puckering bud. She closed her eyes as the invisible connection between her breasts and her belly tingled with aching warmth. One of his hands glided beneath the waistband of her underdrawers, brushing over the curls of her mound. His fingers dipped between her legs. With an involuntary movement, she parted her thighs, and he slid his fingers in her naked moistness.

His chest pressed against her back. She could feel the rough texture of his hair against her. Trembling with the glide of his fingers, she reached behind and pushed his trousers off his hips. With barely a pause, he stepped out of his clothing and she felt the full glory of his sex touch her buttocks, a tantalisingly rock-hard shape. As her hand closed over him, he angled her head and took her lips with his. While she held his arousal she controlled him, but while he teased hers she understood she was equally captured.

His mouth slid against hers as each of his hands gently caressed her. She wanted him, wanted to experience his satin smooth hardness inside her. His lips lifted momentarily and he took a long, deep breath. His hands stilled. Very briefly she tightened her fingers around his heavy length, stimulated by his arching rigidity and the thought of how he would expand and possess her. And how, for a moment in time, she would own him as well.

He steered her towards her bed, his body against hers. He would no more give up their closeness than she would. The hand between her legs pushed her underdrawers down and off. Now entirely naked, she felt gloriously female as he leaned over and flicked the covering off the bed. With a scoop of his powerful arms, he dropped her on the sheet, and then stood staring at her while she gazed back up at him. His look heated her as much as her glimpse of his full frontal nakedness.

"You have the body of a farmhand," she said, her eyes skimming over his wide shoulders, his broad chest and his washboard abdomen, noting his erection, standing thickly out of a nest of dark hair and reaching almost to his waist. His long muscled legs completed his image of perfection. She took a breath, truly impressed with the beauty of his male nakedness.

"What would you know about naked farmhands?" His mouth curved into a grin.

"What I've seen." She heard the shake in her voice as she made space on the bed for the large body settling beside her. "I'm not abnormal. I've looked at the workers as I've passed. Only the younger ones take off their shirts."

He smiled. "I suspect they wanted you to look."

She moistened her lips. "Then, I'm glad I made them happy," she said, and immediately wished she hadn't.

He leaned over her and stared into her eyes. "I'm sure you are going to make me happy too." His mouth twisted with a wry grin.

She flung her arms around his neck and pulled him down to her. As their lips met, his hand covered hers over his sex. The excitement building inside her changed to liquid heat. He dropped his head and his mouth found her nipple. As he suckled he lifted one of her legs around his hip. With his fingers, he teased in her moisture again. She arched her back in pleasure, wanting him everywhere at the same time.

His mouth at her breast heightened the sensation between her legs. When he began sweeping movements with his fingers and started to press slowly inside her, she groaned. His rhythmic stimulation made her whole body quiver with excitement. Her thighs tensed. His mouth moved to cover hers, as if wanting to stifle her speech. His fingers circled far too gently. "Guide me,'" he murmured. "Tell me what you want."

She gave a frantic laugh. "More."

As if he'd previously been teasing, he found the exact spot instantly with his fingers. Already built to a peak, she shattered, over and over again, making incomprehensible smothered noises that turned into a soft laugh as her body finally relaxed. She clutched at his shoulder and turned her body right into his.

He cupped her behind with his hand, breathing hard and burying his mouth in the juncture between her neck and shoulder. Although he didn't speak, his whole body asked a question.

Her eyes closed and she threaded her hand into his soft hair. "That was marvellous," she said in a voice that sounded like a soft sigh.

Holding himself on one hand, he moved between her legs. With a slight adjustment of his hips, he pushed a little way inside her, pressed a little deeper, drew back and eased forward again.

She tried to relax but couldn't. Her knees clasped his hips. "Are you sure you want to do this?"

He gave a slow, rumbling laugh. "I couldn't be more sure. Do you want me to stop?"

"I'm scared. Despite the way I act, I'm really not very experienced," she whispered. "If you keep asking questions, I'll start thinking too much."

"We can't have that." His lips lowered to surround hers and his clever, wonderful fingers eased into her moisture.

Again, and with breathtaking ease, he built her to a state of excitement that had her thrashing her head from side to side and clutching at his back. He took control, giving her the opportunity to experience pure gratuitous pleasure and hot slow tears rolling down her cheeks.

Then his blunt erection between her legs began to persuade. Breathing deeply, she relaxed her knees, appreciating the build, the stretch, and the ever-expanding joy. She found a grip on his hard buttocks, and lost herself in the moment. In a flow of glorious moisture, he started to speed up and she exploded inside, again and again and again, her body clenching against his, holding him, doubling her pleasure.

Finally he stilled, hot and sweaty. She wanted to keep him there forever and he stayed until her heartbeat calmed and her grip eased and her hands relaxed on his sweaty back. She laughed. Only then did he ease out of her. He rolled to the side of the bed and sat up, giving her a perfect view of his wide back.

She leaned over and circled her arms around his shoulders from behind. "I hope you enjoyed that as much as I did."

He spun around and took her into a fiercely protective hold. His chin pressed so hard into the top of her head that it hurt. "Daisy, I love you."

And when he lifted his legs to the bed again and rolled her into his grip, she clung tightly to him. "I love you too, Ash."

Chapter Fourteen

Ash awoke at dawn and discovered that his new wife slept with her palm under her cheek. The early morning light streaming through the lace curtain cast a pattern on her skin. Although he was tempted to touch her soft eyelashes, he refrained. He didn't want to wake her yet.

Last night, her lack of virginal timidity surprised him, though he hadn't really known what to expect, since he'd never been married before. He just hadn't expected such an enthusiastic response to his overtures. For every single kiss he gave her, she gave him two. For his every smoothing of her skin, she made a tentative exploration of him. When he took the final step and had tried to ease into her, she had grabbed his buttocks, and all thought of restraint died. She'd said she was ready, and she hadn't lied.

He praised the Lord for having blessed him with her as his wife. For a man who used to trip over when someone he admired spoke to him, who stuttered if he didn't think about his words before he said them, who'd been tired, tired of being saddled with debts, other people's children, and tired of not managing, she was perfect, no tricks, no salacious offers, simply a wonderful, supportive and appreciative partner.

He rubbed his fingers over his stubble, not able to imagine wanting anyone but Daisy. Asleep, she exuded peace. Awake, she radiated energy and self-possession. More of thinker than a doer himself, he had always admired these qualities. In Daisy he had found them all. He would no more change a hair on her head than stop appreciating her. "I love you," he whispered into her ear, tucking up a lock of her fine hair.

Her eyes opened. She blinked blearily at him and smiled. "Mm?"

"Do you always look so messy in the morning?" He smiled tenderly, smoothing a thumb across her cheek.

"Yes, I do," she murmured in a purring voice. Like a cat in the sunshine, she moved languidly into him, spreading her fingers on his back.

He stared at the delicious lashes on her cheeks, the shiny sweep of her hair and the achingly soft mouth out of which he wanted to kiss words of love. He needed to hear she loved him, too. He scooped her hair off her face with two palms. "Is it too soon to make love to you again."

She glanced at him and widened her sleepy eyes. "But you said I look messy."

"I like messes."

"I hope that doesn't mean you're going to stop shaving every morning," she offered him a mischievous smile.

"My valet would have conniptions if I did."

"And, of course, you are a pink of the ton."

He eyed her suspiciously. "I think you just tried to side-track me."

She blinked with mock innocence. "From what?"

"This," he said in an aching voice, pulling the sheet down, exposing his and her full nakedness. "This lovely body." Knowing that unspoken feelings can't hold any power, he took in the sight of her curves, complimented by her straight shoulders that narrowed down to her waist and long legs. His new wife was no powdered and pampered courtesan. He wondered how he could have wasted so many years on women he had no intention of marrying.

He enclosed her in his arms. Her delicious body moved right up against his. Her mouth sought his. While he gently moved his lips over her face, she glided her hands sensuously over his back.

His kisses grew urgent. Although she seemed a little shyer in the morning sunlight, she soon began to throw away her inhibitions. With her, he wanted the smiles, the intimacies, and the sharing of thoughts and desires. Since he had lured her with his kisses, he planned be the sort of husband a young wife needed: enthusiastic but not demanding, caring but not overly possessive, and ready and able to toss her into bed if she gave the slightest sign of wanting him.

He took his time entering her, letting her guide the pace, and was rewarded by the gift of her frantic clutching, passionate words of love, and the final explosion that expressed how much he had pleased her. In the aftermath, she slept again in his arms.

❧

After two shockingly decadent days at the inn with her new husband, Daisy travelled back to the country house. As the new Lady Ashford, she would have many responsibilities. She assumed she could cope, since she had lived for a while under the wing of Mrs. Toddington, who planned to move back to her old home. Rather than mourning losing the her old position as the mistress of the house, she seemed to be delighted not to act as Ash's hostess any longer.

None of the servants seemed the least surprised to see Daisy wed to Ash, but she suspected that the news had travelled faster than she and her husband. Smithson welcomed her with a deep curtsey, which was wonderful to see. But even more wonderful was having Smithson's undivided attention.

After she'd changed into her morning gown, and had her hair refreshed by the genius of hairdos, she flopped into a chair in the morning room, trying to look exhausted. Ash gave her a sigh of impatience, followed by one of his delicious smiles. He had turned into the pattern-card of an indulgent husband. She couldn't believe she had won the heart of the beautiful and kind-hearted lord.

"Do you think you will miss the girls?" she asked him as she noticed him tapping his fingers on his knee.

"I miss them already, but they should be with their mother." He lowered his amazing eyelashes, imitating a casual demeanour, but after spending seven full nights in his bed, she knew full well the man didn't have single innocent bone in his body. "I could help you try to make a replacement," he said, staring straight into her eyes.

Not about to fall for another of his little tricks to get her back into bed, she firmed her mouth. Well, not quite.

Making love with him had become her favourite pastime. "Do you think we'll have time before dinner?"

"Trust me," he said, rising to his feet. "If there is one thing I can make time for, it's the woman I love. You, my messy, annoying, outspoken adorable wife." Then he held out his arms for a hug.

Also by Virginia Taylor

Spring of Love Series

Forever Delighted

Forever Amused

Forever Heartfelt

More from Serenade Publishing

Brigadier Station Series

By Sarah Williams:

The Brothers of Brigadier Station

The Sky over Brigadier Station

The Legacies of Brigadier Station

Christmas at Brigadier Station (An Outback Christmas Novella)

The Outback Governess (A Sweet Outback Novella)

Heart of the Hinterland Series

By Sarah Williams:

The Dairy Farmer's Daughter

Their Perfect Blend

Beyond the Barre

About the Author

After training at the South Australian School of Art, Virginia accepted a job at an advertising agency. With a more interesting working life in mind, she retrained as a nurse, and then a midwife. By then, she met the man of her dreams, married, had two children, worked part time, and began writing romance.